DEAD DRAW

Fargo's keen eyes spotted the man called Dunkle lifting his revolver. Fargo's hand dipped toward his Colt. Outdrawing a man who already had his gun out was impossible, but Dunkle had to hesitate as the Ovaro lunged between him and Fargo. That split second gave Fargo all the time he needed to catch up. The Colt bucked against his palm as the two shots sounded as one.

Dunkle's bullet whipped past Fargo's ear. Fargo's slug, however, found its target. Dunkle rocked back in the saddle as the bullet drove into his chest. One hand clutched the saddle horn, but the fingers slipped off as he pitched to the ground and landed in a crumpled heap. . . .

THE TRAILSMAN

#248

SIX-GUN JUSTICE

by

Jon Sharpe

A SIGNET BOOK

SIGNET
Published by New American Library, a division of
Penguin Putnam Inc., 375 Hudson Street,
New York, New York 10014, U.S.A.
Penguin Books Ltd, 80 Strand,
London WC2R 0RL, England
Penguin Books Australia Ltd, Ringwood,
Victoria, Australia
Penguin Books Canada Ltd, 10 Alcorn Avenue,
Toronto, Ontario, Canada M4V 3B2
Penguin Books (N.Z.) Ltd, 182–190 Wairau Road,
Auckland 10, New Zealand

Penguin Books Ltd, Registered Offices:
Harmondsworth, Middlesex, England

First published by Signet, an imprint of New American Library,
a division of Penguin Putnam Inc.

First Printing, June 2002
10 9 8 7 6 5 4 3 2 1

The first chapter of this title originally appeared in *Seven Devils Slaughter*,
the two hundred forty-seventh volume in this series.

Ⓥ REGISTERED TRADEMARK—MARCA REGISTRADA

Printed in the United States of America

PUBLISHER'S NOTE
This is a work of fiction. Names, characters, places, and incidents either are
the product of the author's imagination or are used fictitiously, and any
resemblance to actual persons, living or dead, events, or locales is entirely
coincidental.

BOOKS ARE AVAILABLE AT QUANTITY DISCOUNTS WHEN USED TO PROMOTE
PRODUCTS OR SERVICES. FOR INFORMATION PLEASE WRITE TO PREMIUM
MARKETING DIVISION, PENGUIN PUTNAM INC., 375 HUDSON STREET, NEW YORK,
NEW YORK 10014.

The Trailsman

Beginnings . . . they bend the tree and they mark
the man. Skye Fargo was born when he was eigh-
teen. Terror was his midwife, vengeance his first
cry. Killing spawned Skye Fargo, ruthless, cold-
blooded murder. Out of the acrid smoke of gun-
powder still hanging in the air, he rose, cried out
a promise never forgotten.

The Trailsman they began to call him all
across the West: searcher, scout, hunter, the man
who could see where others only looked, his
skills for hire but not his soul, the man who lived
each day to the fullest, yet trailed each tomorrow. Skye Fargo, the Trailsman, the seeker who
could take the wildness of a land and the wanting
of a woman and make them his own.

Northern California, 1860—
Where the lust for gold brings greed and dishonor
and the muzzle of a gun brings the swiftest
of justice.

1

An eagle wheeled through the sky far overhead, and Skye Fargo reined the Ovaro to a halt to watch. His lake-blue eyes shone with appreciation of the scene's beauty. Not only the eagle, this Northern California landscape itself was one of the prettiest things Fargo had ever witnessed. The highest, snowcapped peaks of the Sierra Nevadas loomed over smaller mountains whose slopes were covered with thick, blue-green forests of pine and cedar and spruce. Fast-running, sparkling creeks twisted through the valleys. Over all of it was the blue vault of the sky, dotted here and there with puffy white clouds. Fargo thumbed back his hat and smiled. He patted the sleek black shoulder of the Ovaro. Up here in the high country, it was hard to tell that man had ever touched this land.

Then Fargo stiffened as gunshots began to blast in the distance.

He should have known better than to start thinking about how pristine and untouched this land was. He knew good and well that a little over a dozen years earlier, thousands of men had flooded into Northern California, drawn by the lure of gold. Ever since James Marshall had noticed something shining in the waters of the creek beside Sutter's Mill, nothing had been the same here.

Fargo listened to the shots, his keen ears picking up the sounds of at least three different weapons. From the way the reports were spaced, he could tell that one person was fighting back against several. He had ridden into the Sierra Nevadas just a couple of days earlier, so he had no idea who was doing the shooting, but he knew he didn't like the odds. He heeled the Ovaro into motion and headed down the slope of the hill on which he had paused.

There was a road at the bottom of the hill. Fargo turned

1

to the north and urged the horse into a faster gait, just short of a gallop. He didn't want to ride blindly into what was sure to be a dangerous setting. As he drew closer to the sound of shooting, he eased the Colt into its holster on his right hip, then drew the Henry rifle from its sheath attached to his saddle.

The road took a sharp turn and plunged down to cross a creek at the bottom of a little draw. A wooden bridge spanned the creek, or at least it would have if someone had not come along and chopped holes in the timbers. At the side of the road just short of the bridge, a buggy with a black canopy lay on its side. The wheel that was on the top of the overturned buggy was still spinning. One of the mules hitched to the buggy was down, motionless and probably dead. The other was still in its harness.

Fargo surveyed the scene as he pulled the Ovaro to a stop. He saw puffs of gunsmoke coming from behind a cluster of rocks on the creek bank, not far from the ruined bridge. Whoever had been in the wrecked buggy must have taken refuge there. More shots came from the trees along the slope to Fargo's right. Those would be the bushwhackers, Fargo decided.

To his eyes, the story told by what he saw was clear as day. The bushwhackers had chopped holes in the bridge, then opened fire on the buggy as it started down the hill. The buggy's driver hadn't seen the ruined bridge until it was too late to stop without wrecking the vehicle. He must have been thrown clear in the crash, and he had scurried into the rocks, forting up there to put up a fight.

Even without knowing the driver of the buggy, Fargo was certain whose side he was on in this fight. He swung a buckskin-clad leg over the Ovaro's back and dropped to the ground.

Holding the Henry slanted across his chest, Fargo moved into the trees. Rifles cracked and pistols barked as the bushwhackers continued to pour lead down at their intended victim. From the bottom of the slope, a heavier roar sounded as the man in the rocks fought back. He was using an old percussion pistol, Fargo judged, and the gun wouldn't be very effective against the sort of odds he faced.

Fargo was going to do what he could to even those odds.

He spotted a man crouched behind a tree, firing a pistol

down toward the creek. Fargo stopped and took aim, then squeezed the trigger of the Henry. The rifle bucked against his shoulder. He saw the bushwhacker's hat fly into the air and heard the startled yelp that the man let out. Then Fargo was on the move again, darting behind the thick trunk of a tall pine.

He crouched and used the underbrush for cover as he worked his way along the slope. The man whose hat he had shot off yelled, "Hey! There's somebody else up here!"

Fargo bellied down onto the ground as he located another of the bushwhackers. The man was between a couple of rocks. From this angle, Fargo didn't have a clean shot at him. But there was more than one way to skin a catamount.

Fargo snugged the butt of the Henry against his shoulder and began to fire as fast as he could work the rifle's lever. The slugs smashed into one of the rocks that hid the second bushwhacker and ricocheted into the space between the boulders. The gunman howled in surprise and fear, and the narrow part of his body that Fargo could see disappeared from view as the man hunted for better cover.

Something crashed through the brush behind Fargo. He rolled over and reached down with his right hand to palm the Colt from its holster. He saw a flicker of black and white through a gap in the brush and recognized it as a cowhide vest. Fargo triggered two quick shots in that direction, then rolled again and came up on his feet. He darted behind a tree as bullets smacked into the trunk, sending slivers of bark flying into the air.

"Who is that son of a bitch?" one of the bushwhackers shouted.

"I don't know! I never got a good look at him!"

Fargo holstered the Colt and got on his hands and knees to crawl along the slope. He came to a sharp drop-off and slid down it, landing in some fallen pine boughs at the bottom. He worked back toward the road a short distance, then picked up a broken branch and flung it through the air so that it made a racket in the undergrowth to his left. When the bushwhackers fired toward the sound, Fargo sent three fast shots screaming through the trees around them.

"There's more than one of them! Damn it, I'm gettin' out of here."

He heard more sounds of men struggling through the

3

thick undergrowth. If he had wanted to, tracking them would have been no trouble. But he was content to let the three men go. He had spoiled their ambush without being forced to kill anyone, and rescuing the driver of the wrecked buggy was all he had set out to do.

Fargo waited until he heard hoofbeats receding in the distance. Then he waited some more, just to make sure the bushwhackers weren't trying some sort of trick. When he was satisfied they were really gone, he walked back to the road and whistled for the Ovaro. The horse came trotting down the hill to him.

Fargo slid the Henry into its sheath and took hold of the Ovaro's reins. As he led the black-and-white horse down the hill, he called, "Hey! You in the rocks! Those gunmen are gone!"

The percussion pistol boomed, and Fargo came to a sudden stop as a heavy slug kicked up dirt in the road about twenty feet ahead of him. "Don't you come no closer, dadgum it!" an elderly man's voice shouted from the rocks on the creek bank. "How do I know you ain't one o' those varmints your ownself?"

Fargo stayed where he was, not wanting to tempt a trigger-happy old-timer into shooting at him again. He kept his hands in plain sight and said, "I'm the one who ran them off. Didn't you hear me shooting at them?"

"I heard a bunch o' shootin', but you can't tell which side a gun's on by listenin' to it."

He had a point there, Fargo admitted to himself. "All right, I can't prove it. But if I was one of the men who were trying to kill you, would I be standing out here in the open like this?"

"Maybe, if you was a tricky enough bastard."

"All right," Fargo called. "Reckon I can just mount up and ride away and leave you here. But you'll have a hell of a time getting that buggy back on its wheels by yourself." He turned away from the creek, gathered up the Ovaro's reins, and put a foot in the stirrup, ready to swing up into the saddle.

"Wait just a dadblasted minute!" the old-timer shouted from the rocks. "There ain't no need to be so damned touchy!"

Fargo took his foot out of the stirrup and waited. A

moment later, a man in a dusty black suit and hat emerged from the rocks on the creek bank. Long white hair fell almost to his shoulders, and a bristly white beard covered his jutting chin. He held an old Dragoon Colt in his right hand and used the weapon to wave Fargo closer.

Leading the Ovaro, Fargo walked on down to the ruined bridge. The old man made his way along the creek bank and met Fargo there. Rheumy eyes studied Fargo's muscular six-foot frame and ruggedly handsome features. The old-timer said, "You don't look like no bushwhacker I ever seen."

"That's because I'm not. Name's Skye Fargo."

The old man grunted in surprise. "The Trailsman?"

"That's right."

"I heard of you. You're supposed to be able to track a grain o' sand through a dust storm."

Fargo laughed. "I wouldn't go so far as to say that."

"Never heard anything about Skye Fargo bein' a dirty damned back-shootin' killer, though, so I reckon I can trust you." The old-timer stuck out his hand. "I'm Judge Jameson Boothe, ridin' the circuit from Sacramento."

Fargo had decided already that the old man was either a judge or a preacher. That explained the sober black suit, the white shirt, and the black string tie. Boothe didn't talk much like a judge, but Fargo knew that out here on the frontier, jurists weren't exactly like their counterparts back East. It was a rugged land, and rugged men were needed to settle it. Even a smattering of legal knowledge often qualified a man to be a judge west of the Mississippi.

Fargo shook hands with Boothe, then said, "Looks to me like somebody was trying to stop you from getting to where you're going."

"That's the double-damned truth of it, son. I started ol' Damon and Pythias down the hill, and them hydrophobia skunks opened up on me from the brush. I lit out and never noticed until I was nearly at the bottom that they'd chopped holes in the bridge. That buggy o' mine was gonna wreck one way or the other." Boothe looked at the dead mule and sighed. "Almost wish they'd ventilated me instead o' poor ol' Pythias. He was a damned fine mule."

Fargo commiserated in silence for a moment over Boothe's loss, then said, "Where are you bound, Judge?"

"Headed for a settlement called Ophir. Ever heard of it?"

Fargo frowned in thought. "The name sounds familiar. Wasn't it a boomtown back during the Gold Rush?"

"Sure was. Some o' those forty-niners took a heap o' gold dust and nuggets out of there. Then the color sort of played out for a long time. Now there's rumors floatin' around that a big strike's been made up there, and folks are flockin' in again. You know what that means."

Fargo nodded. He knew, all right. All it took was a hint that gold had been found, or was about to be found, and men hungry for wealth would descend on a place from all over. And not only prospectors and miners, but also all the hangers-on who came with them: gamblers, saloon owners, soiled doves, bullies, gunmen, killers who would murder a man in the blink of an eye. The dregs of civilization. Most of the miners were honest, upstanding men, even though temporarily blinded by their lust for gold. But those who followed them from camp to camp, boomtown to boomtown, were anything but honest and upstanding.

"The decent citizens of Ophir sent word of their troubles to Sacramento," Judge Boothe went on. "They asked the state for help, and I reckon I'm the answer."

"You'll have a big job on your hands," Fargo said. "There'll be a certain element in the settlement that won't want any sort of law and order established."

"You ain't tellin' me nothin' I don't already know, son. I reckon that's why them scurvy bastards've tried to kill me more'n once since I left Sacramento."

Fargo frowned. "This ambush today wasn't the first time someone's tried to kill you?"

"Nope. I managed to outrun 'em twice before." Boothe gave a regretful laugh. "Them mules o' mine can run faster than anybody would think they could, just by lookin' at 'em. I reckon that's why the skunks decided to get in front of me and set up an ambush this time."

Fargo nodded in agreement. "Makes sense, all right. What are you going to do now, Judge?"

"Why, go on to Ophir, of course! I ain't never shirked my judicial responsibilities before, and I'll be damned for a low-down polecat if I start now!"

Fargo gestured toward the bridge. "We can get your

buggy upright, but it won't make it across there. And the creek's too deep and fast for you to ford it."

Boothe tugged at his beard and frowned in thought. After a moment, he said, "I reckon you're right. I'll have to unhitch Damon and ride to town on him."

"How much farther is it to Ophir?"

"I figured to get there 'round noon tomorrow."

Fargo glanced up at the sky. There wasn't more than an hour or two of daylight left. Riding the mule might turn out to be slower than using it to pull the buggy. Mules were balky creatures, and most of them didn't like to be ridden. Still, in all likelihood Boothe could reach Ophir before dark the next day, even riding the mule.

"Someone can come out from the settlement and repair the bridge, then bring the buggy on into town," Fargo said. "Why don't you get anything you need out of it while I unhitch the mule?"

Boothe squinted at Fargo and asked, "Are you plannin' on ridin' with me to Ophir, son?"

Fargo grinned. "I was heading in that general direction anyway, and I don't have any place else I have to be. That's one of the advantages of drifting."

"Hmmph. That ain't much of a life for a grown man to be leadin'. I ain't complainin', mind you. I'll be glad for the company, especially if them bushwhackers show up again."

Fargo didn't say anything, but the same possibility had crossed his mind. If someone had tried three times to stop Judge Boothe from reaching Ophir, a fourth attempt wasn't out of the question. And he knew that was why he had come to the decision he had. He felt an instinctive liking for the feisty little jurist, and he didn't want to see any harm come to him.

Less than half an hour later, Fargo led the Ovaro across the bridge, the horse placing its hooves so as to avoid the holes. Boothe followed, tugging on the reins he had fashioned out of the mule's halter. "Come on, you jughead," Boothe urged the mule. "I don't like leavin' Pythias here, neither, but we ain't got no choice."

When they had crossed the bridge, Fargo gave Boothe a boost onto the mule's back, then swung up into his saddle. Leaving the site of the ambush behind, they rode on through the waning afternoon toward Ophir.

7

Fargo realized that night he hadn't been completely al-
truistic in volunteering to accompany Judge Boothe to
Ophir. His supplies were running low, and a supper of
bacon and flapjacks sure beat the jerky and stale biscuits
that he would have had otherwise. Boothe didn't mind
sharing his provisions and even offered Fargo a cigar after
they had eaten. Fargo shook his head and said, "Thanks
anyway, Judge," then leaned back against a fallen log at
the edge of the clearing where they had made camp. He
clasped his hands behind his head, stretched his legs out in
front of him, and sighed in satisfaction. Nearby, the Ovaro
and the judge's mule cropped at the grass.

Boothe used a blazing twig from the fire to light his cigar.
When he had puffed it into life, he blew out a cloud of
smoke and said, "Where are you from, Mr. Fargo?"

A faint smile played over Fargo's lips. "Lots of places—
and no place," he said. "I've been riding the trails out here
for quite a spell."

"I'm from St. Louis, myself. Came out to the Shining
Mountains nigh onto thirty years ago to do a little trappin',
and I've been out here, one way or another, ever since."

Fargo indulged his curiosity. "How'd you wind up being
a judge?"

"Well, now, that's an interestin' story. I won a bet." Boothe
smacked his lips over his cigar for a second, then continued.
"One of the other trappers, a fella named Newcomb, bet me
once at a rendezvous that I couldn't read. Well, sir, I had me
some schoolin' back in St. Louis, so I knew damn well I could
read. One o' the other fellas had a book . . . don't know
where he'd got it . . . so he gave it to me to read out loud
to Newcomb. I did, and turned out it was a law book. Mighty
interestin' stuff. I decided I wanted to learn more about it,
so the next time I had a load of plews ready to sell, I brung
'em all the way down the Big Muddy to St. Louis instead
o' goin' to the rendezvous. I got me some more law books
whilst I was there and took 'em back to the mountains with
me, where I commenced to study 'em." Boothe inhaled on
the cigar, then blew a perfect smoke ring. "And that's how
I come to be a lawyer. I settled down in Sacramento, and
after a spell they asked me to be a judge."

Fargo nodded. He had no trouble accepting the story

Boothe had just told him. Back East such a progression, from fur trapper to lawyer to judge, would be pretty far-fetched, but out here in the West, such things were common. A man's background seldom stopped him from doing anything he had the talent and the determination to do.

"How about you?" Boothe asked. "How'd you come to break trails all over the frontier?"

"Just something I always had a knack for, I reckon," Fargo said.

"Close-mouthed sort of fella, eh? Well, that's all right. I probably talk enough for two people, myself, so it balances out. Sure you don't want a see-gar?"

"No, thanks."

"Reckon I'll turn in, then."

Boothe rolled up in the bedroll he had taken from the overturned buggy, and soon his snores were making the needles on nearby pine trees tremble. At least, Fargo thought with a grin, the snoring was almost loud enough to do that. He stood up and moved away from the campfire into the trees, taking his rifle with him. He found a good place well out of the diminishing circle of light cast by the campfire as it burned down and settled himself on the ground with his back against a tree trunk. He could doze this way, yet a part of him would stay alert. If anyone came skulking around the camp, Fargo would sense the intruder. So would the Ovaro, and Fargo knew from experience he could count on the big stallion to trumpet a warning if any strangers got too close.

Fargo tipped his hat down over his eyes as he sat there cross-legged with the Henry across his lap, and the night passed quietly.

Even though it was summer, the nights up here in the Sierras were chilly. A cup of hot coffee tasted mighty good the next morning as Fargo hunkered on his heels next to the fire and sipped the strong black brew. "Sleep all right?" he asked the judge.

"I always sleep fine when there ain't nobody shootin' at me," Boothe replied. "I hope that holds true the rest of the way to Ophir. I know one thing: If I ever get the varmint who shot Pythias into my courtroom, I'm goin' to throw the dadblamed book at the son of a bitch!"

9

The two of them were back on the road not long after sunrise. The road, which was little more than a trail, dipped and climbed as it made its meandering way through the mountains and valleys. The sun rose higher, banishing the last of the night's chill, but the air was still crisp and clean, just the way Fargo liked it. His senses were alert for trouble, knowing that the bushwhackers could try to set up another ambush for the judge, but that didn't mean Fargo couldn't appreciate the beauty of the verdant landscape around them.

By midmorning, Boothe was mouthing bitter complaints about the state of his rump. "Mules are fine for pullin' things," he said, "but there ain't a creature on God's green earth that hurts as much to ride. I feel like I'm perchin' my backside on a damned picket fence. It don't help matters I ain't got no saddle."

"I reckon you can walk," Fargo said.

"All the way to Ophir? No, sir!"

Fargo grinned and only halfway listened to the judge's complaints. It was past midmorning when he reined in at the top of a rise and lifted a hand in a signal for Boothe to do the same.

"What is it?" Boothe asked. "You spot them dadblasted bushwhackers again?"

"No, it's something else." Fargo pointed. "Looks like some more pilgrims having trouble."

Up ahead, the road crossed a saddle between the two rocky hills, and a covered wagon was stopped there, at the edge of the trail. Fargo could tell from the way the wagon sat crooked on the ground that it had lost a rear wheel.

"On their way to Ophir to get rich, I'll bet," the judge said. "Reckon they broke an axle?"

"Maybe the hub nut just came off. Let's ride down and take a look."

"Remember, I got to get to the settlement as soon as I can. I can't be sittin' around tryin' to help out a bunch of immigrants."

"You're welcome to ride on by yourself if you want," Fargo said. As for himself, he didn't intend to leave the people from the wagon stuck out here in the middle of nowhere if there was something he could do to give them a hand.

"I didn't say that," Boothe complained. He hitched the mule into its ungainly walk and followed Fargo down the hill toward the wagon.

The vehicle's occupants saw them coming. A heavyset man was standing beside the wagon, looking at the broken wheel in disgust. A smaller, younger man stood by holding a rifle. Someone else was looking out through the opening at the back of the wagon, above the tailgate, but Fargo couldn't make out who it was.

The two men turned away from the wagon and walked up the trail a little way to meet Fargo and Boothe. As they came closer, Fargo saw the resemblance between them and pegged them for father and son. The younger man was actually a boy, no more than seventeen or so.

"Hello," the man said, lifting a hand. To his son, he added, "Harry, put that rifle down."

The youngster was regarding the newcomers with suspicion. "They could be robbers, Pa." He tightened his grip on the old single-shot rifle he held.

"They don't look like robbers."

Fargo grinned as he brought the Ovaro to a stop. "Actually, we're not," he said. "Fact is, this fella with me is a judge."

"Judge Jameson Boothe," the jurist introduced himself.

"And I'm Skye Fargo. We're headed for Ophir, but we saw you and decided you'd had a little trouble."

"Big trouble," the man said, gloom on his face and in his voice. "The wheel came off and nearly dumped everything out of the wagon."

Fargo swung down from the saddle. "Busted axle? Or did the nut come off the hub?"

"I'm not real sure. . . . I'm afraid I don't know much about wagons."

"Let me take a look."

It required only a second for Fargo to tell that the wagon's rear axle was all right. The nut had slipped off somewhere, allowing the wheel to work its way loose until it came off. Fargo pointed that out, saying, "There's your problem. If you've got a spare nut, or if we can find the one you lost, we can get you going again without much trouble."

"I'm mighty happy to hear you say that, Mr. Fargo,"

the man said. "I was afraid we were stuck out here for good." He held out his hand. "I'm Frank Conway, and that's my boy Harry. The girl in the wagon is my daughter Dinah."

Fargo hadn't forgotten that someone was in the wagon, but whoever it was had withdrawn until they weren't easily visible. Now that he knew it was a young woman, he looked into the wagon bed, smiled, tugged on the brim of his hat, and said, "Hello, ma'am."

Dinah Conway leaned forward, emerging a little from the shadow cast by the canvas cover. She returned Fargo's smile with a shy one of her own. "Hello," she said.

She was nineteen or twenty, Fargo judged, with honey-blond hair that fell in thick waves around a pretty face. He saw the proud thrust of full breasts against the homespun dress she wore. Despite her shyness, her brown eyes held a certain boldness as they examined him, and he returned her look with enough boldness of his own to bring a faint flush to her face.

"We came out here from Illinois," Frank Conway was saying. "I used to own a mercantile store there, but after my wife passed on, I decided it was time for a change. The children and I heard there was still gold to be found here in California, so we figured we'd give it a try."

Fargo thought the Conway youngsters probably hadn't had too much to do with the decision to head West. Chances were, the loss of his wife had prompted Conway to seek a change of scenery. Fargo could understand that. What he couldn't understand was somebody setting out on such a long journey with such a meager knowledge of traveling by wagon. Any experienced traveler would have known right away why the wheel had come off.

Conway would learn, Fargo told himself. The frontier was a harsh teacher at times, but those who survived learned a great deal. "Do you have a spare nut?" he asked.

"I don't rightly know," Conway said. "There's a box of tools and such here under the wagon."

A few minutes of poking around in the wagon box turned up a spare nut. Fargo said, "The men will lift the wagon, and Miss Dinah can slip the wheel back on the hub and tighten the nut."

Judge Boothe put a hand to his back. "I ain't sure my lumbago'll let me do such heavy liftin' . . ."

Dinah Conway climbed down from the wagon. "Why don't you put the wheel on, Judge?" she suggested. "I'll help lift the wagon."

Boothe looked embarrassed. "No, missy, that's all right. I reckon my back'll stand the strain just fine if it don't take too long."

Dinah took the nut from Fargo and went to stand beside the wheel. "I'll be ready," she promised.

Now that he could get a better look at Dinah, Fargo saw that she was as lovely as he'd first thought. A little below medium height, her body had lush curves and a grace of movement that was very appealing. Her eyes shone with intelligence. Fargo thought that he would like to get to know her better, but first things first. That meant getting the wagon fixed and rolling on toward Ophir.

After the heaviest items had been unloaded from the wagon, Fargo placed himself at the rear corner nearest to the missing wheel. "Judge, you get here in the middle of the tailgate. Mr. Conway, you and Harry take the side there, just ahead of the wheel."

Everyone got in position and took a good grip on the wagon. Fargo looked at Dinah. "Ready?"

She nodded. "Ready, Mr. Fargo."

"All right . . . *Lift!*"

With grunts of effort, the men strained to raise the vehicle. Although immigrant wagons were built with as little metal as possible so they would be lighter in weight, they were still heavy. Fargo shifted his feet a little and threw more of his strength into the task. The corner of the wagon came up off the ground. Slowly, the men raised it until the axle was level again.

"Now," Fargo panted. "Get the wheel on!"

Dinah grabbed hold of the iron-rimmed wheel and brought it upright. Clutching the spokes, she wrestled it into position. The wheel itself wasn't light, and Dinah had to struggle to maneuver it in place. When the axle was protruding through the hub, she moved fast to get the nut on. Spinning it with deft fingers, she tightened it to hold the wheel in place.

"All right," Fargo said to the men. "Ease it down and step back."

They did so, and as the wagon's weight came down on the wheel, the nut held.

"You'll need to tighten that better with the wrench that's in the box," Fargo told Conway. "Once you've done that, it'll get you to Ophir with no trouble."

"I can't thank you enough, Mr. Fargo," Conway said. "You, too, Judge." He looked at Fargo again. "Can Harry and Dinah start loading our goods back in?"

Fargo nodded. "I'll give them a hand."

Judge Boothe rubbed his hands together and said, "I was wonderin', Mr. Conway, if to show your appreciation you might see your way clear to lettin' me ride the rest of the way to Ophir on this here wagon? That mule o' mine has the boniest spine this side of the divide."

"Why, sure, Judge," Conway answered without hesitation. "If you need a ride, we'll be glad to give you one. You didn't have to help."

"Oh, I didn't mind."

Fargo smiled to himself. Now that Boothe had a ride, he wasn't worried about his lumbago anymore.

In another ten minutes, the nut had been tightened, the wagon had been reloaded, and everyone was ready to go. The judge's mule Damon was tied onto the back of the wagon, and Boothe climbed up next to Frank Conway. Dinah and Harry rode in the back of the wagon. Fargo led off, keeping the Ovaro at an easy walk.

Things sure could change in a hurry, he reflected as he rode along. Less than twenty-four hours earlier, he had been traveling alone through the Sierras. Now he had plenty of company. He looked up at the sun. Still plenty of time to reach Ophir today, he decided.

When they stopped for the noon meal, Conway insisted on sharing his family's provisions with Fargo and Judge Boothe. "There should be plenty of supplies to be had in Ophir," he said.

"Yes, but the storekeepers will be wantin' a pretty price for them," Boothe warned. "You might should've stayed in the mercantile business instead of decidin' to be a prospector, Conway."

Conway shook his head. "No, keeping a store isn't for

14

me anymore. I want to do something more exciting than that."

Fargo had never thought of prospecting as being particularly exciting. But then, he had always been content with the simple things in life: a good horse, a trail to follow, the heavens overhead. That was enough for him.

After lunch, the little group started on toward Ophir. Fargo suspected that they were nearing the settlement when the road got a little wider and smoother. He wasn't expecting what they found just around a bend, however.

Six men, tough-looking and gun-hung, sat there on horseback blocking the trail.

2

Fargo brought the Ovaro to a halt and motioned for Frank Conway to do the same with the wagon. Conway pulled back on the reins and called, "Whoa," to the team of draft horses. Fargo didn't take his eyes off the men in the road, especially the one who walked his horse forward a couple of steps, assuming the role of the group's leader.

"Howdy," the man said. "Bound for Ophir, are you?" He was burly and barrel-chested, with a prominent, beard-stubbled jaw.

"That's right," Fargo said. "Are we on the right road?" He knew they were, but he wanted to hear what the man would say in answer to the question.

"Oh, yeah, you sure are. This trail will lead you right into town, 'bout a mile farther on. You can't miss it."

"Much obliged for the information," Fargo said. He hitched the Ovaro forward a step. "Now, if you fellas could just move out of the way for a minute . . ."

The spokesman shook his head. "Well, now, we can't quite do that. You see, we're here on business." He waved his left hand at the trail, while keeping his right close to the walnut grip of the revolver holstered at his hip. "This is a toll road, and you folks will have to pay if you want to follow it on into Ophir."

"A toll road?" Frank Conway repeated. "I didn't know there were any toll roads around here."

Fargo wished Conway had kept his mouth shut instead of revealing just how green he was, but it was too late now. "It's not a toll road," Fargo said.

That made the leader of the gunmen frown. He leaned forward in the saddle. "You wouldn't be callin' me a liar, now would you, mister?"

"Maybe you're just on the wrong road," Fargo said, his voice cold. "Or you picked the wrong pilgrims to stop."

From behind him, Conway said, "Mr. Fargo, we're not looking for any trouble."

Fargo could understand why Conway sounded nervous. The man had his children with him, after all, and he was more worried about their safety than anything else. But at the same time, Conway had to understand what they had run up against in these gunmen. Demanding the payment of a toll was extortion, pure and simple, and Fargo wasn't going to stand for it. He knew good and well this was a public road.

One of the other men said, "Hell, Gratton, you gonna let him talk to you like that?"

Fargo's gaze flicked over to the speaker for a second, and his eyes narrowed as he saw that the man was wearing a black-and-white cowhide vest. Fargo hadn't forgotten what had happened the day before. During the brief fight with the men who had ambushed Judge Boothe, he'd gotten a glimpse of just such a vest. That didn't prove this man was one of the bushwhackers—there had to be more than one vest like that in Northern California—but it seemed likely to Fargo that he had been.

"Shut up, Dunkle," the man called Gratton said. Fargo could tell that his pride was wounded. Gratton glared at him and went on, "Look, mister, this is a toll road if I say it is. Pay up, or turn that wagon around and get the hell out of here!"

Conway began, "Maybe we should—"

Fargo heeled the Ovaro forward even more, bringing himself closer to Gratton. "Stay out of it, Frank," he said over his shoulder. "This is between Gratton and me."

Gratton's lips drew back from his teeth in a snarl. He was reacting just as Fargo hoped he would. By putting this on a personal level, between the two of them, he hoped that the other men would leave Judge Boothe and the Conways alone.

"You think you're the big he-wolf of these parts, don't you?" Fargo said. "You think that you've got everybody buffaloed. Sorry, Gratton, but you picked the wrong partner for dancin'."

"Just who the hell do you think *you* are? I heard that pilgrim call you Fargo, but I don't know any Fargo except . . ." His voice faded as realization dawned in his eyes.

With a tight smile, Fargo said, "That's right. My name's Skye Fargo."

Dunkle, the gunman in the cowhide vest, let out a low whistle. "He's the one they call the Trailsman, Gratton."

"I know who he is, damn it!" Gratton snapped. "And I don't care. He's still got to pay the toll if he wants to ride past." He wiped the back of his left hand across his mouth. "How about it, Mr. High-and-Mighty Trailsman? You ready to dance?"

"Any time you say, Gratton."

Fargo wasn't sure what to expect. He thought that Gratton might reach for his gun. Instead, the burly tough took him by surprise. With a yell, Gratton kicked his feet out of the stirrups and flung himself from the saddle in a diving tackle that sent him slamming into Fargo.

Fargo grabbed for the saddle horn but missed. He felt himself falling, and a second later he crashed to the ground with Gratton on top of him. The impact knocked the breath out of Fargo's lungs. For a second, his head swam and he gasped for air. He brought a knee up and drove it into Gratton's midsection, then heaved the man off him, knowing that he had to buy a little time or else he might black out.

If that happened, Gratton might well beat him to death. The man was filled with a killing rage, and Judge Boothe and the Conways wouldn't be able to stop him.

Fargo rolled to his right and came up on his knees. A few feet away, Gratton struggled up from the ground and came at Fargo, swinging a wild punch just as Fargo gained his feet.

Gratton's hamlike fist tore through the air above Fargo's head as the Trailsman ducked the blow. Fargo bored in and hooked a left and a right to Gratton's belly. Hot breath laden with the smell of stale whiskey burst from Gratton's mouth into Fargo's face and made him grimace. Fargo jabbed a left to the other man's nose, then brought his right fist up from his knees in a perfectly timed uppercut that sledged into Gratton's jaw. The burly gunman was lifted up and back by the punch and fell sprawling under the hooves of his horse. He let out a yell of fear as he realized how close he was to being trampled.

Several of the men with Gratton were off their horses now. They rushed forward. One of them grabbed the reins of Gratton's mount, skittish from the fracas, and tried to bring the animal under control. Two more dragged Gratton out of harm's way. Fargo stepped back, fists still clenched. His heart was pounding in his chest, but he felt good. It had been very satisfying to knock a bully like Gratton into the dirt.

"Fargo, look out!" Judge Boothe shouted.

Knowing that any threat was likely to come from Gratton's companions, Fargo's instincts pivoted him toward the remaining gunmen, rather than toward the wagon. His keen eyes spotted the man called Dunkle lifting a revolver. Fargo's hand dipped toward his Colt. Outdrawing a man who already had a gun in his hand was just about impossible, but Dunkle had to hesitate as the Ovaro lunged between him and Fargo. That split second gave Fargo all the time he needed to catch up. The Colt bucked against his palm as two shots sounded as one.

Dunkle's bullet whipped past Fargo's ear to bury itself in the road behind him. Fargo's slug, though, found its target. Dunkle rocked back in the saddle as the bullet drove into his chest. One hand clutched the saddle horn, but his fingers slipped off as Dunkle swayed to his right. He tried to get off another shot, but failed. He pitched to the ground and lay in a crumpled heap.

Fargo shifted his aim to cover the other men. "Anybody else want to take cards in this game?" he asked, his voice harsh.

None of the men reached for their weapons. They kept their hands motionless and in plain sight instead.

"You bastard!" Gratton was on his feet now, shaking his head as he stood there supported by the two men who had pulled him away from the horse. "You killed him!"

"Wasn't time to do anything else," Fargo said. "Looks like he's the one who paid your toll, Gratton."

"You won't get away with this!"

From beside the wagon, Harry Conway said, "I reckon he will, mister. You'd better do like Mr. Fargo says and clear out."

The youngster's voice held a surprising tone of authority. Fargo wasn't surprised when a glance told him it was backed up by the rifle in Harry's hands. The rifle was only a single-shot, but Harry handled it with a practiced ease that indicated his lone bullet would no doubt go exactly where he wanted it to go.

"Harry, blast it—" Conway began.

"It's all right, Pa. I know what I'm doing."

"So do I," Judge Boothe put in as he hefted the Dragoon Colt he had taken from its holster under his coat. "Any o' you boys want to have a talk with this old hogleg of mine, you just go right ahead."

"Ah, the hell with this!" Gratton said as he pulled away from the men supporting him. He picked up his hat and knocked the dust off of it against his leg. "Put Dunkle back on his horse, and let's get out of here."

Fargo was watchful for any tricks as the gunmen threw Dunkle's body across his saddle and lashed it in place. Still looking a little groggy, Gratton mounted up and turned a baleful glare on Fargo.

"This ain't over," he warned.

"Anytime you want to finish it, you know where to find me," Fargo said. "I'm going to Ophir."

Of course, he reminded himself, he hadn't planned to stay all that long in the settlement. What a man figured on didn't always turn out that way. Fargo had a feeling that once he reached Ophir, leaving might not be as easy as he'd thought it would be.

Gratton and the other gunmen wheeled their mounts and rode away, leading the horse that carried Dunkle's corpse. Fargo waited until they were out of sight before he holstered his gun and picked up his hat.

Frank Conway looked pale and shaken. "I'm sorry you got mixed up in that, Mr. Fargo. We should have just paid the toll and gone on—"

"Damn it, Pa!" Harry burst out. "Mr. Fargo was right. This ain't a toll road. Those men were thieves."

"Maybe so, but a man was killed—"

"He was a grown man, Conway," Fargo said. "It was his

choice to reach for a gun. Besides that, I think he may have been one of the men who tried to murder the judge yesterday."

Boothe blinked and stared at Fargo. "What's that? What's that you say? That fella was one o' them gol-durned bushwhackers?"

"He could have been. When I was trading shots with them in the woods, I caught a glimpse of a cowhide vest like the one Dunkle was wearing. I never got a good enough look at the bushwhacker to be sure, but I'd be willing to bet it was the same man."

"What's this about an ambush, Judge?" Conway asked.

"Seems there's somebody who don't want me goin' to Ophir," Boothe explained. "They've tried three times to stop me."

"Why would anybody do such a thing?"

Fargo walked to the Ovaro and gathered up the horse's reins. "Somebody in Ophir doesn't want the judge bringing law and order to the settlement," he said in answer to Conway's question. "They have a stake in seeing that Ophir remains lawless. Could be we just met the man responsible for the ambushes, too."

Boothe looked at Fargo. "You're talkin' about that fella Gratton?"

"He was in charge of this bunch. Whether or not he's taking orders from somebody else, I don't know yet."

"Sounds like you intend to find out."

"Maybe," Fargo said. "It depends on what kind of reception's waiting for us when we get there."

The rest of the trip into Ophir was uneventful. Fargo was alert, in case a vengeful Gratton and his companions were lying in wait, but he saw no sign of them.

Ophir lay in a shallow valley between two long ridges that ran north and south. The settlement had one main street and several short cross streets. Since the town had been in existence for over a decade, it had a sizable number of permanent buildings, rather than being composed mainly of tents and tar-paper shacks as most boomtowns were. Ophir might have looked like that in its early days, but not now. The main street was crowded with wagons, buggies, horses, mules, and pedestrians. The boardwalks that lined the streets were packed as well. A creek ran to the west of the settlement and curved across the road below it to meander over to the east side of the valley. The road crossed the stream on a substantial bridge of heavy beams and thick planks.

As Fargo rode across the bridge, he looked up and down both sides of the street in front of him. He saw the usual blend of general stores, saloons, hotels, boarding houses, blacksmiths, livery stables, gunsmiths, and all the other staples of a frontier town. There were more saloons and mercantiles than normal, however, and he knew that was a result of gold-hungry miners pouring into the area. Those prospectors would want supplies and liquor, not necessarily in that order. There would be quite a few whorehouses in town, too, but those establishments didn't advertise their presence quite so openly.

He led the Conways' wagon past the assay office and noted that next door was a doctor's office. The next business they passed was a large general store with a loading dock out front that was an entire block long. A big sign proclaimed the place to be SPRAGUE'S EMPORIUM—OMAR SPRAGUE, PROP.—MERCHANDISE FOR EVERY NEED. On the opposite corner was the Alhambra Saloon. Across the street were the Top-Notch Saloon and the Ace-High Saloon, then the Royale, the Crystal Palace, Beeker's Saloon, Drummond's Gold Bar, and several more drinking and gambling halls. There was a shooting gallery, a row of beaneries and hash houses, a laundry, and even a millinery shop with a glass window that must have been freighted in at great expense from San Francisco. Fargo recalled hearing that after the Gold Rush of '49 was over, Ophir had almost dried up and blown away. Most of the commercial development he was seeing now must have happened in the past few months. That came as no surprise. Entire towns could spring up almost overnight once rumors of a gold strike started going around. Ophir had had a head start since the settlement already existed.

"I didn't know there would be so many people here," Frank Conway said from the wagon seat. "It's almost like back home."

Fargo doubted that. Ophir might have a thin veneer of

civilization over it, but it wasn't like Illinois. You could scratch the surface of almost any place west of the Mississippi and find trouble.

Fargo stopped in front of the Drake Hotel, which was a solid-looking building of whitewashed planks. It had an actual second floor, not just a false front to give it that appearance. Quite a few horses were tied at the hitch racks. Fargo swung down from the saddle and added the Ovaro to that number.

"I don't know where you folks plan to sleep tonight," he said, "but I think I could use an actual bed for a change."

Conway rubbed his jaw. "I don't know that we can afford a hotel room. We spent most of our money on the supplies we'd need to come out here."

"We can camp outside of town, Pa," Dinah said. "We've spent so many nights under this wagon, one more won't make a difference."

Harry added, "Maybe tomorrow we can stake a claim and start building a cabin." His voice was full of controlled excitement.

Judge Boothe climbed down from the wagon seat. "As for me," he said, "I reckon I need to find whoever's in charge around here. The mayor, I suppose. I expect they can tell me in the hotel where to find him."

He and Fargo climbed the three steps to the hotel's front porch. From the wagon, Conway said, "We're much obliged for all your help, Mr. Fargo. You, too, Judge. We'll see you around later."

Fargo nodded. He felt a little bad about turning Conway, Harry, and Dinah loose to fend for themselves, but they had to start learning how to deal with their own problems. Besides, he reminded himself, they had made it all the way from Illinois to within a day's ride of their destination. That was proof right there that they weren't helpless, just inexperienced.

Dinah looked over her father's shoulder and called, "Good-bye, Mr. Fargo. Thank you."

Fargo smiled and waved as Conway got the wagon moving again, heading north along the street. Judge Boothe smacked his lips and said, "That there's a mighty pretty gal."

"You mean Dinah? I can't argue with you, Judge."

"The way she was lookin' at you, she wouldn't be at all upset if you was to come callin' on her, Fargo."

"We'll see," Fargo said without committing to anything.

He and the judge went through double doors into the hotel lobby. The slick-haired clerk behind the counter greeted them with a smile. "Howdy, gentlemen," he said. "Welcome to the Drake Hotel." He directed most of his attention toward Judge Boothe. Fargo supposed the judge looked more respectable to the clerk than he did in his dusty, well-worn buckskins.

The judge smiled back at the clerk. "I'm Jameson Boothe, circuit court judge from Sacramento. Whereabouts will I find the mayor o' this burg?"

The clerk looked impressed but sounded somewhat chagrined as he said, "We, uh, don't have a mayor, Judge. I've heard there used to be a town council and a mayor here, back when Ophir was a boomtown the first time, but there ain't been nothin' like that around here for quite a while."

"No mayor, eh? I wonder who it was that sent for me, then."

"Oh, that'd be Doc Parkhurst, I reckon. He was the first one to start sayin' that we need a judge here in Ophir to bring us some law and order. I seem to remember hearin' that he'd wrote a letter to the capital askin' for help."

"Parkhurst, eh?" Boothe said.

"I saw his office back down the street," Fargo put in. "I'll walk down there with you, Judge, as soon as we get checked in."

"You gents want rooms?" the clerk asked. "Don't have much available. Only one room, in fact, and if you want it, you'll have to double up with a Russian fella who's already stayin' in it."

Fargo thought about it for a second, recalling that there were several decent-looking livery stables in town. He could bunk in whichever of them he chose for the Ovaro. A pile of straw wouldn't be as good as the real bed he had been looking forward to, but he figured the judge would appreciate the bed even more.

"You take the room, Judge," he said. "Don't worry about me."

Boothe frowned. "You're sure?"

"Certain."

"I appreciate that, Fargo. These old bones o' mine are mighty stiff from sleepin' on the ground durin' the trip out here."

Boothe signed the register, then he and Fargo left the hotel to walk down the street to Dr. Parkhurst's office. As they went along the boardwalk, Fargo saw that most of the other pedestrians were men, many of them in the rough garb of prospectors, a few in town clothes. There were only a handful of women, and most of them were painted up so that their profession was obvious. Several of the soiled doves eyed Fargo as they strolled past, and he smiled and nodded to them in return.

Angry voices coming from across the street drew Fargo's attention. He looked over and saw two men standing on the boardwalk shouting insults at each other. One of them wore a floppy-brimmed felt hat, flannel shirt, overalls, and work boots. The other was dressed in tight, brown whipcord trousers, a cutaway coat, silk shirt, and a brown beaver hat. He sported what looked like a diamond stickpin in his cravat. Fargo knew the fancy-dressed man had to be a gambler, while the other man was a prospector.

"—nothin' but a no-good cheat!" the prospector yelled, and Fargo expected to see the gambler reach for a gun. The man turned pale with anger but didn't make a move.

"Then stay out of the Gold Bar," the gambler said. "You're too much of an oaf to play cards anyway."

"I'll show you, you damned lowdown—" The prospector stabbed a hand at one of the pockets of his overalls.

Fargo caught hold of Boothe's arm, knowing that lead was about to fly. "Watch out, Judge!"

All along the block on both sides of the street, people yelled in alarm and ducked for cover as the gambler and the prospector went for their guns. The gambler's weapon was a derringer that seemed to appear in his hand as if by magic. Fargo's eyes were quick enough to see the little gun slide out of the holster strapped to the gambler's forearm and hidden under the sleeve of his coat. The prospector's draw was a lot slower, since he had to haul a good-sized pistol out of a deep pocket. But he had reached for his gun first, so that made this a fair fight, at least in the eyes of the law and established custom.

The gambler's derringer cracked sharply. Flame and smoke belched from the muzzle of the gun. At distances over five feet, derringers were so inaccurate as to be almost useless, but the barrel was less than a foot from the prospector's chest when the gun went off. The prospector took a sudden step backward and struggled to lift his gun. Before he could do so, the gambler shifted his aim and used the derringer's second barrel to shoot the man in the middle of the forehead.

The prospector's head snapped back and his knees buckled. He fell to his knees, dropping the gun in his hand on the boardwalk. With blood welling from the black-rimmed hole in his forehead, he pitched forward onto his face.

"Good Lord," Judge Boothe said. "A killin' in broad daylight!"

Fargo had a feeling the judge wasn't really as surprised as he sounded. Given Boothe's background, he probably had seen plenty of shootings in the past.

The citizens of Ophir didn't seem too disturbed by what had happened. Once the shooting was over, they came out of the hiding places they had ducked into and went on about their business while the gambler calmly reloaded his derringer and tucked it away in his sleeve holster. Meanwhile, a small pool of blood formed around the head of the dead man.

Fargo and Boothe had almost reached the doctor's office. Now, in response to the gunshots, the building's front door opened and a man came bustling out. He was short, stocky, and middle-aged, and he had a derby hat pushed back on his curly brown hair. He clutched a black leather bag in his right hand as he hurried across the street, pushing between pedestrians and dodging men on horseback. When he reached the opposite boardwalk, he exchanged a few low-voiced words with the gambler, who then turned and strolled uptown. The doctor bent over the dead man, rolled him onto his back, then straightened up and gave a heavy sigh. He shook his head as he started back across the street.

Fargo and Boothe were waiting for him. "Doc Parkhurst?" Boothe asked.

"That's right." Parkhurst looked at the judge. "And who might you be?"

"I might be the Queen o' England, but what I am is the

26

circuit court judge you folks here in Ophir sent for. Judge Jameson Boothe."

The weariness on Parkhurst's face disappeared. He transferred his medical bag to his left hand, then reached out with his right and caught hold of Boothe's hand. As he pumped it, he said, "I'm mighty glad to meet you, Judge. You can see for yourself how badly we're in need of some law around here." He inclined his head toward the dead man still lying on the opposite boardwalk.

"What are you going to do with that fella?" Fargo asked.

"Oh, the undertaker will be along in a minute," Parkhurst said. "I used to have that job, too, but thank goodness somebody else came along and took it over. It's hard enough to lose a patient, but it's even worse when you have to plant 'em, too." He looked Fargo up and down. "Who might you—no, wait a minute. Who are you, sir? Not the Queen of England, I trust?"

"Not hardly. Name's Skye Fargo."

"I'm pleased to meet you, Mr. Fargo. Are you traveling with Judge Boothe here?"

"Just since yesterday," Fargo said. "We ran into each other on the trail."

"What Fargo ain't tellin' you is that he saved my bacon from a bunch o' murderin' bushwhackers," Boothe said.

Parkhurst's bushy eyebrows went up in surprise. "Someone tried to ambush you? That's terrible!"

"Yeah, I thought so the first two times the polecats tried it." Boothe gestured toward Parkhurst's office. "Why don't we go inside, and I'll tell you all about it. Then you can tell me about the troubles you got here in Ophir. You wouldn't happen to have any medicinal alcohol in there, would you?"

Parkhurst smiled. "I think I might be able to find a bottle. Come on, gentlemen."

A few minutes later, the three men were settled in Parkhurst's office. The doctor sat behind a desk cluttered with papers, books, glass jars holding what looked like pieces of various human organs floating in clear liquid, and a complete human skull. Boothe took a leather chair in front of the desk, while Fargo sat on a battered sofa along one wall. Parkhurst dug around in a desk drawer and came up with a bottle of whiskey and three jars like the ones on his desk that held organ specimens. Fargo wasn't sure what had been in the jars to start with, but he figured if the whiskey was potent enough, it would kill anything that might have been left behind.

"To your health, gentlemen," Parkhurst said when he had poured and passed around the drinks. He tossed back a slug and licked his lips in appreciation.

"That fella across the street didn't have a very healthy day," Fargo said. He sipped the whiskey and felt it burn all the way down his gullet.

"Ned Simmons. Quite a hothead, he was. And a terrible card player. I take it he accused Tom Harlin of cheating."

Boothe nodded. "Yep. I figured the tinhorn would go for his gun right then and there, but he didn't. That fella Simmons drew first."

Parkhurst nodded and sighed. "That makes it a fair fight and a legal killing, even though in reality Ned never had a chance."

Fargo said, "Harlin works at the Gold Bar saloon?"

"That's right. Walt Drummond's place. You know him, Mr. Fargo?"

Fargo shook his head. "I don't know anybody here except the judge and the folks we rode into town with. Family named Conway."

"Newcomers, eh? Welcome to the crowd. Not a day goes by that half a dozen new people don't show up in Ophir, come to make their fortunes."

"Is there really a gold strike?" Boothe asked.

"Fresh color's been found on several claims up the creek. Not enough to make anybody rich yet, mind you, but the signs are encouraging if you're after gold. And it seems like everybody is, these days."

Fargo wasn't, but he didn't bother explaining that.

Judge Boothe and Dr. Parkhurst talked for several minutes about conditions in the settlement. In the past six weeks, Parkhurst said, there had been twenty killings either in town or up the creek in the valley. Those were the deaths that he knew of, there could have been others. In addition, there had been countless fights and beatings and nonfatal stabbings and shootings, not to mention daily robberies. Fargo had seen such patterns of lawlessness in other boomtowns. Sometimes vigilantes rose to put a stop to it, but often the only thing that could be done was to let the violence play itself out. That was frustrating to those who considered themselves civilized men, and Parkhurst was the embodiment of that frustration.

"I can establish a court," Boothe said, "but the citizens will have to do their part. First thing will be to organize a town council and elect a mayor. Once that's done, you can hire a marshal. I don't expect you get much help from the county sheriff, out here in the sticks the way you are."

Parkhurst made a sound of disgust. "I haven't seen the sheriff around here since he was running for re-election. That's always the way it is."

"Yeah. You might as well gimme some names of gents you think might be willin' to serve as councilmen. Then we'll go talk to 'em."

Fargo didn't have any interest in helping Boothe with this organizational work. The judge and Parkhurst could handle that. Fargo got to his feet and said, "I think I'll take a walk around town, Judge. I need to get my horse stabled, too."

Boothe was still concentrating on the plans he was making with Parkhurst. He gave Fargo a distracted wave and said, "Fine. See you later, son."

Fargo left the doctor's office and walked back up the street. He untied the Ovaro from the hitch rack in front of the Drake Hotel and led the big black-and-white stallion toward one of the livery stables. Several people gave the Ovaro stares of admiration. With most horses, a fella might have to worry about thieves in a place like this. Not the Ovaro. Anybody who tried to steal him ran a good chance of winding up with his head kicked in.

Fargo was used to people admiring his mount, but even so he was a little surprised when a voice said from the boardwalk, "My God, what a magnificent animal. Whatever your price is, I'll buy him."

The voice belonged to a woman, and when Fargo looked over at her, he saw that she was beautiful. She wore an expensive and stylish blue gown, and a feathered hat of the same shade perched on a mass of thick black curls. She was even carrying a parasol. She looked like she ought to be walking along the streets of San Francisco or Paris, rather than a gold-mining boomtown in the Sierra Nevadas.

Lovely or not, her attitude rubbed Fargo the wrong way. He said, "The horse isn't for sale."

"Come now," the woman said. "Everything has its price."

"Not this horse—and not me."

Something flared in the woman's dark eyes. "Is that a challenge?"

Fargo hadn't meant it that way, but he realized, looking at her, that it was exactly the way he wanted her to take it.

3

"Only if you want it to be," Fargo said.

"What sort of horse is that?" the woman asked, changing the subject. "I don't think I've ever seen one exactly like it before."

"He's an Ovaro," Fargo replied. He had a feeling she was just trying to prolong the conversation.

"Is he fast?"

"Very."

"Have you ever run him in races?"

"A few times," Fargo said.

"I assume he won?"

"Most of the time. Not always." Fargo smiled. "No matter how fast you are, there's always somebody faster. That applies to horses as well as men."

"And what about women?"

"I wouldn't know about that."

A smile curved her full lips. "I have a feeling you know just about everything there is to know about women . . . especially fast ones."

"Right now all I want to know is which livery stable in town is the best?"

The smile didn't leave her face, but she gave a tiny shake of her head. Not an admission of defeat in this verbal jousting, but rather a postponement of the rest of the game.

"Try Patterson's," she said. "That's where I keep my horse and buggy."

Fargo touched a finger to the brim of his hat. "Much obliged."

"And when you're done there, come down to the Top-Notch. The first drink is on the house."

"You're sort of free with the place's whiskey," Fargo commented.

31

"I can afford to be. I own the saloon."

With that, she spun the parasol over her head and turned away. Fargo watched her stroll along the boardwalk, appreciating the smooth grace with which she moved.

He walked on up the street and in a few minutes found Patterson's livery stable and wagon yard. Patterson was a tall, talkative, gaunt-faced man who promised to take good care of Fargo's horse and for a little extra money was agreeable to letting Fargo bunk in the hayloft.

"Come to Ophir to get rich?" Patterson asked.

"Nope, just happened to be traveling this way and fell in with another pilgrim who was heading here." Fargo paused, then decided to take advantage of the livery owner's garrulousness. Such men usually knew just about everything that was going on in a settlement. "You'll hear about it soon enough, I reckon. A circuit court judge has come to town from Sacramento. Going to set up a court of law here."

Patterson let out a whistle. "Is that so? Well, we sure been needin' one. It's getting so bad, honest folks don't hardly show their faces on the street after dark."

Fargo felt an instinctive liking for the man. "Judge Boothe and Doc Parkhurst are going to be looking for some men to serve on a town council. Would you be interested in the job?"

"I sure would. If you run into 'em, tell 'em to be sure and come see me."

"I'll do that," Fargo promised. "Right now, though, I think I'll head down to the Top-Notch and have a drink. I met a lady who claims to own the place."

"That'd be Natalie Talmadge. Fine-lookin' woman."

"Is the saloon on the up-and-up?" Fargo hadn't forgotten about the attempts to stop Judge Boothe from reaching Ophir. While he suspected Gratton and the other gunmen might have had something to do with the ambush, Gratton could be working for somebody else. A saloon owner who was running crooked poker games or some other illegal activities would have an interest in keeping law and order out of Ophir.

Patterson shrugged in answer to Fargo's question. "I reckon it's as honest a place as any saloon. I never heard about anybody bein' cheated in there, and there ain't as

32

many fights as there are in some of the other places in town."

"Sounds like a man could get a drink of good whiskey, then."

"Just be sure the drink juggler pours it from the bottle under the bar."

Fargo nodded. "Thanks for the advice. I'll see you later."

"I lock up the front doors after dark, but when you're ready to turn in, you can get in the door in the back."

Fargo nodded again and went out. It was late afternoon by now, and the sun was touching the peaks to the west. Lights were beginning to glow in the windows of some of the buildings.

The entrance to the Top-Notch Saloon was at the corner of a block. Fargo pushed through the batwings and went in. It was a little early yet for a crowd, since it wasn't even dusk, but he saw that the saloon was almost full anyway. Poker games were in full swing at most of the tables. A roulette wheel clicked as it spun. Only a few places were open at the bar. Tobacco smoke hung in the air, along with plenty of talk and laughter.

Fargo looked around and didn't see Natalie Talmadge. Three bartenders were working behind the polished mahogany. Fargo drifted in that direction and wedged himself between two prospectors. He rested a boot heel on the brass rail along the bottom of the bar. When the nearest bartender came over, Fargo said, "Whiskey."

The man reached for one of the bottles arranged in a glittering row on the back bar, beneath a long mirror. Fargo said, "Pour it from the bottle under the bar."

The bartender looked at him. "Don't know what you're talkin' about, mister. This is the good stuff, up here."

"I've been told different, and since it was Miss Talmadge who invited me here and told me the first drink was on the house, I'd appreciate it if you'd go along with what I asked for, friend." Fargo's voice was mild, but an underlying tone of steel said that he didn't want an argument.

The bartender hesitated for a second, then shrugged. "Whatever you say, friend." He reached under the bar, took out an unmarked bottle, and splashed amber liquid from it into a glass. "Just for the record, though, it's Mrs. Talmadge, not Miss."

"Thanks," Fargo said. "I didn't know that."

He took the drink and tossed it back. It was a lot smoother than the whiskey he'd had in Doc Parkhurst's office earlier, but it had the same sort of kick to it. As he set the empty glass on the bar, he went on, "Is the lady around this evening?"

"She'll be down in a little bit, I expect." The bartender hefted the bottle. "Another?"

Fargo shook his head. He wanted to keep his thoughts clear. "I'll have a beer instead."

The bartender drew the beer, cut the foam with a wooden paddle, and slid it over to Fargo. "That'll be two bits."

Fargo didn't argue. He dropped a coin on the bar, picked up the mug of beer, and turned to walk around the room, watching several of the poker games for a few minutes each. What Patterson had told him seemed to be true: The games in the Top-Notch were straight. Fargo had a good eye for a card cheat, and he didn't see anything fancy going on.

Several painted women were circulating through the room. They were probably available to take upstairs for a price. Fargo wasn't interested at the moment, but he had to admit that some of the women were quite attractive. All in all, Natalie Talmadge seemed to run a fine place.

He wondered what Mr. Talmadge had to do with it—or if there even was a Mr. Talmadge.

A brief hush fell over the room, and Fargo glanced toward the stairs that led to the second floor, seeing several of the customers doing the same. Natalie Talmadge was descending the stairs. She had changed from the blue dress she had been wearing earlier to a red gown that clung to the curve of her hips and swooped low in the neck to reveal the twin swells of her creamy breasts. She wore no hat now, but her elaborate arrangement of curls was adorned with a red plume that matched her dress. A little gaudy, Fargo decided, but still beautiful.

Several men came up to line the stair railings and speak to her on her way down. She smiled and flirted with them, but there was nothing serious about it. Her gaze moved across the room, landed on Fargo, and stayed there. When she reached the bottom of the stairs, she came straight across the room toward him, the crowd parting before her like the Red Sea before Moses and the Israelites.

"Mr. Fargo," she said as she came up to him. "I'm so glad you could accept my invitation."

Fargo recalled that he hadn't introduced himself to her during their earlier conversation. The fact that she knew his name meant that she had asked some questions about him. Well, turnabout was fair play, he decided. He returned her smile and said, "Thank you for inviting me, Mrs. Talmadge."

She gestured toward the mug in his hand. "Surely you didn't waste your free drink on beer?"

"No, I had some whiskey—from the bottle under the bar."

Natalie laughed. "That's only for special customers. I'd say you fit that description." She linked her arms with his. "Come. Sit with me at my table."

Fargo wasn't going to refuse. He enjoyed the way the soft fullness of her breast pressed against his arm as she led him toward a large round table in one of the rear corners. One of the bartenders was there before they reached the table, pulling out a chair for her and then pouring drinks after they were seated.

"Is supper almost ready, George?" Natalie asked.

"Yes, ma'am," the bartender replied.

"For two?"

"Yes, ma'am, just like you said."

After the bartender left, Natalie smiled at Fargo and said, "I hope you won't think I'm too brazen, assuming that you'll have supper with me like that."

"Not at all. I've been on the trail for quite a while. Something besides jerky and biscuits will taste mighty good. But what's Mr. Talmadge going to eat?"

"It's not a matter of what Mr. Talmadge is eating, but rather what's eating him. Worms, I imagine. He's dead."

"I'm sorry," Fargo said.

"Don't be. He was a thorough bastard. The only reason we got along even part of the time is that I can be just as much of a bitch when I want to be."

"I find that hard to believe."

"Don't waste gallantry on me, Fargo," she said. "I'm a woman who knows what I want, and I don't mind going after it." She put a hand on his where it lay on the table. "As soon as I saw you this afternoon, I knew I wanted you. I'm willing to bet that Ovaro of yours isn't the only stallion around here."

Fargo had to look down at the table for a moment and bite his lip to keep from laughing. She was brazen, all right. He wondered how much of that was an act, a façade she had cultivated because she was a woman trying to make her way in a rugged world full of men.

"Why don't we just have supper and see how things go?" he suggested with a faint smile.

She took his response well. "Of course."

The bartender brought out the meal a few minutes later. Fargo was surprised to see that the main course was baked chicken. A good rooster or laying hen was worth a lot in a boomtown because fresh eggs would fetch a premium price. Natalie was going all out to impress him.

That included leaning forward enough so that he had a good view of her cleavage. Fargo felt himself becoming aroused. He had been a while without a woman, and there was no denying Natalie Talmadge's loveliness. Maybe when they finished eating he would go ahead and take her upstairs to her room, since she had left no doubt in his mind that was what she wanted.

But then one of the other bartenders came over to her, a worried look on his face, and bent down to whisper something in her ear. Natalie tried to control her expression, but Fargo saw the way her features tightened and anger shone in her eyes. Something was wrong.

"What is it?" he asked as the bartender left the table.

"Nothing," Natalie said. She slid her chair back. "Just business. Something I have to check on. You stay here and enjoy the rest of the meal, Skye."

Fargo was on his feet before she was. "What kind of gentleman would I be if I did that? If there's trouble, maybe I can help you."

"Really, it's none of—" She stopped short and shook her head. "There's no point in arguing with you, is there? You're not the sort of man to be told to stay out of something."

"I've been told I'm too curious for my own good," Fargo admitted with a smile.

"Come on, then."

She led the way to an unobtrusive doorway and through it into a rear hall. The short hall led to an office. Waiting inside was a gangling, blond-haired man who was holding a bloodstained rag to his forehead.

"Johnny!" Natalie exclaimed. Her concern for the man was evident to Fargo. "What happened? Al told me there was trouble with the shipment."

The man nodded his bloody head. "Yes, ma'am. They jumped me 'bout five miles out of town."

"Who? Who jumped you?"

"I don't know. They was all masked. One of 'em was up in a tree, and when I drove under it, he dropped on top of me and knocked me off the wagon. They had axes, and they busted up all the kegs so the whiskey and beer run out, and chopped up the wagon wheels and run off the team. I tried to stop 'em, but they clouted me and knocked me out. When I come to, I had to walk on into town."

Natalie looked like she didn't know whether to hug Johnny or chew nails. "Those bastards! They had to be some of Drummond's men."

Johnny nodded again. "Yes, ma'am, that's what I figured, too. Wish I'd got a good look at 'em."

Fargo had been listening to the man's story and thinking about its implications. He said, "What time did this happen?"

Johnny had given him several suspicious looks when he came into the office with Natalie. Now, instead of answering Fargo's question, he said, "I don't reckon I know you, mister."

"He's a friend, Johnny," Natalie said. "I'll vouch for him."

"Well . . . if you say so, Miss Natalie." He looked at Fargo. "I reckon it was around two o'clock this afternoon, give or take a half hour. I was knocked out for a spell, and it took me a good long while to walk on into town."

"Was one of the men who attacked you wearing a black-and-white cowhide vest?"

Johnny started in surprise. "How'd you know that?"

"Because I ran into him later in the day. He's dead now."

Johnny's eyes widened. "Dead? What happened to him?"

"He pulled a gun on me," Fargo said. From another man, the words might have sounded like boasting. From Fargo, they were just a statement of fact.

"I heard something about this," Natalie said. "You were with that judge who came into town today?"

"Judge?" Johnny repeated. "We got us a judge now?"

Natalie ignored him and continued talking to Fargo. "Gratton and his men tried to charge a toll to those people you were with, and you had a fight with Gratton. One of his men was wearing that cowhide vest. Dunkle?"

"That's what they called him," Fargo admitted. "Sounds like Gratton and his bunch are well-known around here."

"We know them better than we want to. They've been suspected of all sorts of things, killings and claim jumpings and the like, but nobody's been able to prove any of it. Anyway, until today there hasn't been any law here to report the crimes to."

"This fella Drummond you mentioned owns the Gold Bar Saloon. Is there a connection between him and Gratton?"

"Drummond says there isn't." Natalie shook her head. "But I don't believe him. Not for a second. I wouldn't believe anything that comes out of that lying bastard's mouth." Fargo could see the anger growing inside Natalie until it could no longer be contained. "In fact, I think it's past time we had a showdown."

With that, she stalked out of the office, paying no heed to Johnny's pleas for her to stay put.

Fargo went after her and caught hold of her arm, knowing that he had no real right to interfere with her business, but unwilling to let her charge full-bore into trouble. "What are you going to do?" he asked.

"I'm going over to the Gold Bar and telling Walt Drummond just what I think of him. I may take an axe and bust up some of his liquor kegs, too!"

"That shipment Gratton and his bunch destroyed—you need it to keep operating?"

Natalie calmed down enough to frown in thought. "No, I can send to San Francisco and have another shipment started on the way up here. My supply may get a little tight, but we'll get through all right unless the whole town decides to get drunk at once—and you can't rule that out."

"So there's no reason to go on the warpath and march over to Drummond's place with fire in your eyes."

"Damn it, Skye, Walt Drummond's been trying to run me out of business ever since I came to Ophir!"

"Let me have a talk with him," Fargo suggested, "since I'm sort of an uninterested third party."

Natalie put her hands on her hips. "You're not interested in me?"

Fargo glanced down at her breasts, which were still rising and falling quickly from the depth of the emotions gripping her. "I'm plenty interested," he told her. "That's why I don't want you to get hurt."

She relaxed a little. "I thought I told you to save the gallantry."

"Nothing gallant about it. I have purely selfish reasons for wanting you to stay healthy, Mrs. Talmadge."

"Why, Mr. Fargo . . ." She nodded as she made up her mind. "All right, go talk to Drummond. But be careful, Skye. He's a lying weasel, and he's a dangerous man. And that Tom Harlin, who runs the games for him, is a killer."

Fargo nodded, recalling that he had seen Harlin in action earlier this evening, when the gambler had gunned down Ned Simmons. "I'm used to keeping my eyes open," he told Natalie.

She stepped closer to him and put her hands on his arms. Her face lifted to his, and her lips pressed to his mouth in a kiss. She tasted hot and wet and sweet. When she stepped back, she said, "There. That'll remind you to come back to me."

"You don't have to worry about that," Fargo said. "I'm not going to forget where to find you."

Drummond's Gold Bar was in the next block, on the same side of the street as the Top-Notch. It had large windows with a lot of fancy gilded curlicues on them, and its sign was bigger than the one on the Top-Notch. Although there were other saloons in Ophir, Fargo could tell that this place would be Natalie's chief competitor. Drummond's saloon appeared to be almost, but not quite, as busy as the Talmadge establishment.

Fargo pushed through the batwings. A piano player was busy tickling the ivories in a corner. Men clad in the rough work clothes of miners and prospectors gambled and drank and talked and laughed and fondled the soiled doves who circulated through the room. A haze of smoke hung in the air. One saloon was much like another, Fargo thought. There were times when he felt an attraction to such places, but more often, they made him long for open skies and fresh air. Tonight was no exception.

Fargo's eyes were drawn to a man who was standing at the far end of the bar that ran down the right side of the room. He was tall and broad-shouldered, and his head was bald despite the fact that he seemed to be only in his thirties. He radiated an aura of brutal power. He was dressed in an expensive suit and silk shirt, but there was still something of the roughneck about him. Fargo's instincts told him he was looking at Walt Drummond.

Drummond was talking to an older, smaller man with bushy side-whiskers and a short goatee. The two of them were arguing, Fargo realized. The smaller man raised a hand and shook a finger in Drummond's face. Drummond looked like he wanted to catch hold of that finger and snap it off, but he restrained himself. As Fargo moved closer, he heard the smaller man saying, "You won't get away with it, Drummond. Haven't you heard? There's going to be law and order here in Ophir."

Drummond laughed, but the sound held little humor. "I've always been a law-abiding man, Omar. You know that."

Fargo remembered where he had seen the name *Omar* before. While it was possible more than one man in Ophir could be dubbed that, Fargo felt it more likely the smaller man was Omar Sprague, the owner of the large mercantile store down the street.

"You tell Gratton I won't stand for him and his hardcases bullying my freighters," the man Fargo assumed to be Sprague went on. "I'm going to hire guards, and the next time anybody tries to stop my wagons, there'll be trouble!"

Drummond dropped his jovial pose and said, "I told you, Sprague, Gratton doesn't work for me. I don't like having him around here any more than you do. And I sure as hell didn't hire him to interfere with you bringing in goods for your store."

Sprague snorted in disbelief. His contempt for Drummond was so obvious, Fargo thought for a second that the saloon owner was going to take a swing at Sprague. But then Drummond just shook his head and said, "Get out."

Sprague didn't look like he intended to move. Fargo took the opportunity to step up beside the storekeeper and say, "Having some trouble here, Mr. Sprague?"

Sprague's eyes darted at Fargo. "Do I know you, sir?" he asked.

"Name's Skye Fargo. I came into town today with Judge Boothe."

Sprague's eyes widened. "You're the man who killed Dunkle!"

The exclamation made things go quiet in the Gold Bar. Talk died away, and after a second the professor at the piano realized something was going on and stopped playing.

Fargo looked at the massive bald man and said, "Drummond, I just came from the Top-Notch. Somebody—probably Gratton and his boys—attacked one of Mrs. Talmadge's employees who was bringing in a wagonload of liquor. They destroyed the shipment and beat up the driver."

Drummond grunted. "Sorry to hear that. But it doesn't have anything to do with me."

"Mrs. Talmadge believes it does. She thinks you hired Gratton to do it." Fargo inclined his head toward Omar Sprague. "Now I hear that Mr. Sprague here has had a similar problem. Maybe you're thinking of going into the mercantile business and want to get rid of your competition, Drummond."

Drummond's fingers curled, as if he longed to clench his hands into fists and could only just restrain the impulse. "I don't like being accused of such things in my own saloon," he said. "I've heard of you, Fargo, but I'm not afraid of you. You don't have any right to come in and start throwing accusations around."

"I'm just trying to get the lay of the land," Fargo said, his voice cool. "You strike me as the ambitious sort, Drummond, the kind of man who'd like to own the whole town, no matter what you had to do to get it."

"You don't know a damned thing about me." Drummond was so angry he was almost snarling. "Get out."

"Mrs. Talmadge is a friend of mine." Though he had

only known Natalie for a short time, Fargo didn't hesitate to make that statement. "If she has any more trouble, I'll be back to see you, Drummond. You'd better remember that."

"If that bitch has trouble, it's none of my lookout."

Fargo had to restrain an impulse of his own then. He wanted to plant a fist in the middle of Drummond's face. But instead he just said, "Remember what I told you," and turned to walk out of the Gold Bar.

Omar Sprague fell in step beside him and left the saloon with him. As they moved along the boardwalk, the storekeeper said, "You're the one they call the Trailsman, aren't you?"

"That's right."

"Thank God! Ophir's been needing a man like you to come in here and clean out the riffraff."

Fargo's long stride stopped short, prompting the smaller man to halt, too. Frowning, Fargo said, "Wait a minute, Sprague. What makes you think I intend to clean out anything or anybody?"

Sprague blinked in surprise, his face showing confusion in the lights that came through building windows. "But . . . but you're working for Judge Boothe, aren't you? He and Doctor Parkhurst came to see me and said that the judge was establishing a court of law here."

"I rode into town with Boothe, but I'm not working for him. I'm not a lawman."

Sprague shook his head. "Then why did you come in there and confront Drummond like that?"

"Because a friend of mine had some trouble and seemed to think that Drummond was behind it. Besides, if I hadn't gone to the Gold Bar, Natalie Talmadge would have, and the mood she was in, I didn't think that was a very good idea."

"Yes, Mrs. Talmadge can be quite, ah, volatile in her temper. You and she are friends, then?"

"We just met today—but I just got to Ophir today, too."

Sprague didn't seem to want to pursue the details of that. Instead, he said, "Mr. Fargo, I'm going to be a member of the town council that's forming, along with Dr. Parkhurst and Joe Patterson and some of the other businessmen in town, and on behalf of the council, I'd like to offer you the job of marshal."

Without hesitation, Fargo shook his head. "I told you, I'm not a lawman. I've worked for them, and I've even pinned on a badge a time or two in the past, but it's not anything I have any interest in doing right now."

"But you're the only man in these parts who's qualified for the job, the only one with nerve enough to stand up to men like Drummond and Gratton. You've proven that!"

"Maybe that's Ophir's problem—not enough men with nerve."

Fargo turned and walked on down the street, ignoring Sprague when the storekeeper called his name again. He went back to the Top-Notch, and as soon as he came into the saloon, Natalie hurried over from the bar where she had been standing.

"Did you see Drummond?" she asked. "What happened? I didn't hear any shots, but I was worried . . ."

"Drummond claims he didn't have anything to do with what happened to your driver," Fargo said.

"You didn't believe him, did you? I told you he's a liar."

"He didn't seem very trustworthy, especially since there was somebody else there accusing him of doing pretty much the same thing. Gratton has been interfering with the shipment of goods to Omar Sprague's store, too."

"Sprague was in the Gold Bar arguing with Drummond?"

"That's right."

"I'm not surprised, Skye. I'm convinced that Drummond wants to have a finger in every pie in this settlement, no matter what it takes."

"I got pretty much the same impression," Fargo agreed. "I told Drummond that if it happens again, I'll be back to see him."

Natalie nodded. "Thank you. It may not do any good, but I appreciate the effort. And it's probably a good thing you stopped me from going up there. If I had, there would have been a brawl. I can see that, now that I've calmed down a little."

Fargo smiled. "I wouldn't want you getting into a fight. Might bruise that beautiful face of yours."

She returned the smile, but she looked distracted. "Thank you, Skye. I'm sorry our supper was interrupted. I'm afraid the food's all cold by now."

"That's all right."

"And I'm afraid that I'm not in any mood for . . . well, for anything else."

"That's all right," Fargo said again, though he felt a twinge of disappointment this time. "I understand that you're upset."

"It's just that I've worked so hard to make this place a success, and then to have somebody like Drummond come along—" She stopped and shook her head. "Complaining doesn't do any good, does it? I think I'm going to call it a night." She came up on her toes and brushed her lips across Fargo's, seemingly heedless that there were dozens of men in the saloon who were watching and who would probably kill for one of her kisses. "Another time," she whispered.

Fargo nodded. "Another time."

Natalie turned and walked to the stairs with nearly every pair of male eyes in the place following her, including Fargo's. No matter where she was or what she was doing, men would look at her. She possessed that sort of classic beauty.

With a sigh, Fargo turned back to the bar and asked for whiskey. This time the bartender poured it from the special bottle without being asked.

Fargo stayed in the Top-Notch just long enough to finish the drink, then left and walked up the street to Patterson's livery stable. As the stableman had said, the big double doors in the front of the barn were closed. Fargo went to the back of the building. He heard snoring as he passed a small window and figured that Patterson's personal quarters were back here. He moved on to a door, tried it, and found it unlocked. Moving with his customary quietness, Fargo went inside.

One candle was burning on a shelf near the tack room, casting a feeble glow that allowed Fargo to find his way around the stable. He glanced in at the Ovaro as he passed the stallion's stall and saw that there was plenty of straw, as well as grain in the feed bin and fresh water in the trough. The Ovaro blew air through its nose and reached its head over the stall door to nuzzle Fargo's shoulder.

Fargo rubbed the horse's nose for a moment, then headed for the ladder that led up to the hayloft.

He climbed to the top of the ladder and stepped off onto the planks that made up the floor of the hayloft. As he did so, something moved in front of him. He heard the soft scuff of a shoe or boot against the boards, and someone took a sharply indrawn breath.

Fargo didn't wait to see what was going to happen. A man could wind up dead that way. Instead he lowered his head and threw himself forward, crashing into whoever was lurking in the loft and driving the person back into a pile of hay. The two of them slammed to the floor, their landing cushioned somewhat by the hay. Fargo pushed himself up on his left hand and cocked his right fist, ready to throw a punch.

That was when he realized the body he was lying on top of was soft, curved, and unmistakably female.

4

"Oh, my goodness!"

Fargo thought he recognized the voice that uttered that breathless exclamation. "Dinah?" he asked.

"Mr. Fargo? Thank God it's you. I was afraid . . . well, I didn't know what to think."

Fargo pushed himself up and off of her. He got to his feet, fished a match out of the pocket of his buckskin shirt, and used a thumbnail to snap the lucifer into life. The sulfurous glare showed him Dinah Conway sitting on the floor of the loft, picking pieces of straw out of her thick, honey-blond hair.

"Dinah, what in blazes are you doing here?" Fargo asked. He looked around, found a lantern hanging on the wall, and lit it while he waited for her answer.

She stood up and brushed off the seat of her long brown skirt. She wore a white shirt with puffy sleeves. The top button was unbuttoned, revealing the smooth, tanned skin of her throat and just a hint of the valley between her high, full breasts.

"I came to see you, of course," she said.

"How did you know where to find me?" Fargo hadn't seen any of the Conways since parting company with them at the Drake Hotel that afternoon. A lot had happened since then.

"I went to the hotel and spoke to Judge Boothe. He told me you'd said you would stay in the livery stable where you left your horse. After that, it was just a matter of finding that Ovaro of yours. That wasn't difficult."

Fargo supposed it wasn't. The big black-and-white stallion was one of the finest specimens of horseflesh in the entire settlement, maybe *the* finest. People tended to remember horses like that. All Dinah would have had to do was ask around at the various stables.

"Did Patterson tell you I was staying up here in the loft?"

"Yes, he did. That's all right, isn't it? He seems like a nice man. I don't want you being angry with him."

Fargo was a little irritated, but the feeling passed almost instantly. He chuckled and said, "No, I'm not angry. I reckon Joe could tell you didn't mean me any harm." Fargo paused, then went on, "But why *are* you here?"

"I told you, I came to see you. There's something I wanted to do . . ."

"What?"

She stepped closer to him, put her arms around his neck, and said, "This." Raising herself on her toes, she brought her lips up to his and kissed him.

Instinct sent Fargo's arms around Dinah's waist. He caught her to him, feeling the solid warmth of her body as she molded it to his muscular form. His manhood began to harden against her soft belly. Her lips parted to allow his tongue to probe into her mouth. He moved his hands down to the rounded curves of her backside. She made a little noise deep in her throat as she thrust her pelvis against him.

It was a very enjoyable kiss, and Fargo liked having her in his arms. But he was a little hesitant and she must have sensed it, because she pulled back a little and whispered, "What's wrong?"

"I'm friends with your father and your brother," Fargo pointed out.

"Aren't you friends with me, too?" Dinah asked.

"I'd sure like to think so."

"Well, what's wrong with a man and a woman sharing a friendly kiss?"

Her ample breasts were flattened against his chest, and he could feel her erect nipples prodding against the thin fabric of her shirt. He said, "This is more than a friendly kiss, Dinah. You know that."

"What I know," she said, "is that ever since I met you, Skye Fargo, I've wanted to strip those buckskins off of you and feel every inch of that body. I know it's brazen to talk that way, but I don't care. I want you!"

She took her right arm from around his neck and reached between his legs with that hand. Her fingers closed over the thick shaft that jutted out from his groin and massaged it through the buckskin.

"You want me, too," she said. "I can tell."

Under the circumstances, it would have been foolish for him to deny that he was aroused. She was right—he wanted her. But he still had reservations. He didn't want to take Dinah for a roll in the hay—literally—and then have her get the wrong idea about how things would be between them.

She must have sensed his hesitation, because she said, "If you're worried about me being some sort of blushing virgin, don't be. I've been romping with boys since I was fifteen. Shoot, most of the girls I knew back home were married by that age."

She had a point there, Fargo thought. She knew what she wanted, and her self-assurance told him this wasn't the first time she had gone after it. He leaned back enough so that he could cup her left breast in his right hand. She pushed her groin against him again as he squeezed the soft flesh and thumbed the hard nipple.

After a moment, his fingers went to the buttons of her shirt. Fargo flipped them open and spread the shirt wide. The soft light from the lantern made Dinah's skin glow as Fargo exposed both of her breasts. The nipples were large brown circles. He leaned down and drew the right one into his mouth, sucking on it as she stroked his head and swayed back and forth a little.

"That's wonderful, Skye," she said, her voice growing hoarse from the desire building inside her. "That feels so good."

Fargo moved over to the other breast and ran the tip of his tongue around the pebbled bud. Then he opened his mouth wide and swallowed as much of the creamy flesh as he could. He reached behind her, under the skirt, and rubbed the bare skin at the small of her back. She whimpered as he slid his fingers under the waistband of her skirt and began to work it down over her hips. She wore nothing under the skirt. When it fell around her ankles, she stepped out of it and stood before him clad only in the open shirt and high-topped shoes. Fargo thought her body was beautiful, all soft, rounded, sweeping curves. The triangle of hair between her thighs was thick and a shade darker than that on her head. Fargo ran his fingers through it, then cupped her mound and pressed the base of his hand against her. She thrust back against his touch. His middle finger found her wet vagina and plunged into it. Dinah gasped as he penetrated her.

Fargo put his left arm around her waist to support her as he lowered her onto the pile of hay. He was still sliding his finger in and out of her. Her juices were already flooding out of her as she lay back and parted her thighs to make it easier for him to caress her. She closed her eyes and sighed in contentment, then stiffened in surprise as he lowered his head between her legs and slid his tongue between the folds of feminine flesh.

"Skye!" she cried out. "Oh, my God!"

Fargo kept licking and stroking her as her hips bucked up off the floor and her thighs clamped around his head. He slipped his hands under her rump to steady her. Her climax rolled through her in a series of jerks and spasms. When she relaxed at last, she shuddered from the depths of her being at what she had just experienced.

Fargo was hard as a rock. He straightened up and peeled the buckskin shirt over his head, then stripped off the trousers. He moved back over Dinah, poising himself between her widespread thighs. As the tip of his shaft touched her opening, she looked up at him and whispered, "Oh, yes, Skye, fill me up!"

With a thrust of his hips, he buried himself inside her. She wrapped her muscular legs around him and met his thrusts as he began to pump in and out of her. With each stroke, he withdrew until he was almost out of her, then plunged forward so that he was sheathed fully once again. His hips rose and fell in the timeless rhythm that drove both of them higher and higher toward the crest that would mark the culmination of their passion.

When Fargo couldn't hold back any longer, he drove into her so that he was lodged as deeply as possible. He began to spasm as his climax boiled up and exploded from his shaft in spurt after white-hot spurt. He emptied himself inside Dinah, filling her to overflowing. She climaxed at the same time, mingling her outpouring of juices with his.

Fargo was so drained that for a moment all he could do was lie there on top of her, supporting some of his weight with his elbows so that he wouldn't crush her. Dinah kept her legs wrapped around his hips and her arms around his waist, so that he couldn't have gone anywhere even if he had wanted to. His organ softened and slipped out of her, and she made a little sound of loss. Then Fargo rolled off of her and sprawled on the hay beside her. He put his arms around her and drew her against him, snuggling her into his side as she rested her head on his shoulder. The sweet fragrance of her hair filled his nostrils.

"I never . . . I never felt anything like that," she said at last. "I just thought those other boys knew what they were doing. I was wrong."

Fargo gave a quiet laugh. "Folks have to move along at their own pace. They get better with practice, most of the time, no matter what it is they're doing."

"Maybe so, but there wasn't a blasted one of them who ever thought to do what you did, you know, with your mouth. Skye, that was just so . . . so . . . I don't know how to describe it. The only thing wrong was that I didn't get to return the favor."

"There'll be other chances," Fargo told her. Practicality intruded itself on his mind, whether it was welcome at this moment or not. "Where's your wagon?"

"We camped just north of the settlement, beside the creek."

"What about your father and Harry? Aren't they going to miss you?"

Dinah laughed. "They were both sawing wood when I left. Once they're good and asleep, those two don't wake up for anything short of an earthquake. So I can stay here a while longer, if that's what you're thinking about." She reached over and cradled his shaft in the palm of her hand. Even soft, it was long and thick, and as she caressed it, the pole of male flesh began to grow and stiffen. "Already?" she asked in surprise.

"Like I told you," Fargo said with a smile, "other chances."

Dinah returned the smile as she lifted herself over him and turned so that she could bring the head of his shaft to her mouth. Her lips opened and took it in, and Fargo closed his eyes in pleasure as he felt the heat of her mouth enclose him.

It had been a long, eventful day, and it looked like it was going to be a long night, too. But Fargo thought he could manage to keep going for a while . . .

Dinah left the stable well before morning. Fargo insisted on walking her back to the spot where Frank Conway had camped the night before. The air was quite cool, and despite his tiredness, Fargo felt refreshed.

"Pa plans to go on up the valley today and look for a good spot to stake our claim," Dinah said as she and Fargo walked along the creek under the stars.

"How's he going to know the place when he finds it?" Fargo asked.

"Do you mean does he know anything about prospecting?" Dinah laughed. "He read some books about the Gold Rush before we started out here. And he's talked to everybody we've run into on the way and asked them what they know about hunting for gold. He has a lot of ideas. To tell you the truth, I don't know, Skye. But he's my father, and I'll do whatever he thinks is best."

Fargo admired her loyalty to Conway, but he worried that the former storekeeper from Illinois would be out of his depth here in California. He made a mental note to take a look for himself at the location Conway picked out for a claim. Maybe if it wasn't a good one, Fargo could nudge the man into trying somewhere else.

They reached the grove of trees where the wagon was parked. Fargo heard the two sets of snoring that came from underneath the vehicle. Dinah was right—her father and brother weren't likely to be disturbed by her coming and going. He kissed her good night, a tender moment that summed up everything that had passed between them, then watched her until she had climbed into the wagon. Smiling, Fargo turned back toward Ophir.

Back in the loft of the livery stable, he slept for several hours, the deep, dreamless, invigorating slumber of a man at peace with himself. He didn't wake up until the sun had risen and its rays were slanting in through the opening at the far end of the loft. As Fargo sat up, yawned, and stretched, he heard Patterson moving around down below.

The liveryman greeted Fargo with a grin. "Sleep good?" Patterson asked.

"Just fine," Fargo replied, not explaining that it had been quite late before he finally got the chance to doze off.

"Judge Boothe's called a meetin' for this mornin' down at Sprague's store," Patterson went on. "He wants ever'-body who's agreed to be on the town council to get together and figure out what to do next. He asked me to tell you that you're invited."

Fargo frowned. He wasn't going to be a member of the town council, he wasn't anything but a man passing through. The Trailsman had no desire to be appointed town marshal or any other official post in Ophir, or anywhere else. He had been happy to rescue the judge from those bushwhackers and see that he got where he was going, but that should have been the end of it.

Of course, there was that run-in with Gratton to consider, and the lead-swapping session with Dunkle that had left the gunman dead. On top of that was the encounter with Walt Drummond and the possibility that the owner of the Gold Bar was responsible for much of the lawlessness plaguing the area. Like a spider spinning a web, fate was casting strands around him, Fargo thought, that would make it hard for him to turn his back on Ophir and ride away.

"If I see the judge, what do you want me to tell him?" Patterson asked.

"Tell him I'll be there if I can," Fargo said. "First, though, I want some breakfast."

Patterson recommended one of the hash houses, and Fargo strolled down the street to find it. After a meal of strong black coffee, fluffy biscuits with molasses, and thick slices of ham, he felt pretty much human again. When he left the little hole-in-the-wall café, he glanced down the street toward Sprague's emporium. Several men were going into the store, and Fargo recognized Joe Patterson among them. He heaved a sigh. Might as well find out what Judge Boothe had to say, he decided.

When Fargo reached the door of the emporium, he found a hastily scrawled sign posted on it: CLOSED FOR TOWN COUNCIL MEETING. He tried the door and found it unlocked. As he stepped inside, he saw Boothe clambering onto the counter at the rear of the store so that he could address the dozen or so men who were gathered in front of it. Fargo recognized Omar Sprague, Dr. Parkhurst, Joe Patterson, and the clerk from the Drake Hotel, who was probably the owner of it as well. The other men were strangers to him. Some wore suits while others were garbed in work clothes, but all of them had a look of solid respectability about them.

Judge Boothe spotted Fargo and said, "Here he is now, boys. Come on in, Fargo, and throw the latch on that door behind you, so we won't be bothered."

The other men turned to look at Fargo as he snapped the latch on the door. He said, "Go ahead with what you're doing, Judge. Don't mind me."

"Hell, you're one o' the main reasons we're here," Booth said.

Fargo didn't like the sound of that. He went over to a pickle barrel and propped a hip on the lid, leaning there and crossing his arms over his chest.

"All right, this meetin' will come to order," Boothe said, lifting his arms to signal for quiet. The gesture wasn't necessary, because all the other men were looking up at him in silent anticipation. Boothe continued, "This is the first official meetin' of the Ophir Town Council. You men have agreed to serve, so I'm hereby appointin' you until somebody says otherwise. First thing we got to do is decide who's goin' to be the mayor o' this here settlement."

"Can't you be the mayor, Judge?" one of the men asked.

Boothe shook his head and ran his fingers through his beard. "No, sir, I can't. That wouldn't be legal an' proper. I'm an outsider, and you need one of your own for the job."

Omar Sprague began, "If no one else wants it—"

"What about Doc Parkhurst?" Patterson suggested. "I reckon he's got more schoolin' than just about anybody in town, and he gets along with ever'body, too."

Parkhurst held up his hands. "Wait just a minute," he said. "I agreed to serve on a town council. Nobody said anything about being mayor."

"I think it's a good idea," another man said. "I vote for Doc."

"Me, too," a third man chimed in.

Boothe held up his hands again. "Wait just a minute. It's high-handed enough for me to appoint you boys as council members. The mayor's got to be elected by the people, and to have an election, you got to have two gents runnin' for the office. How 'bout Doc Parkhurst and Mr. Sprague here?"

That proposal brought a chorus of agreement and approval. Sprague waited until it died down, then said, "Listen, men, when I started to volunteer a few minutes ago, it was because I thought nobody else was going to. I'd really rather see Doc have the job."

"Aren't any of you listening to me?" Parkhurst asked in mounting frustration. "I don't want the job, either."

"All right, then, it's settled," Boothe said. "Doc and Mr. Sprague will run for mayor, and the town will decide. May the best man win!"

Shouts and applause went up from the others. Parkhurst and Sprague both looked overwhelmed, as if realizing there was nothing they could do to stem this tide. They exchanged a glance, and Sprague shrugged.

"All right, all right," Boothe went on when the little celebration died down. "Now on to our second order o' business, and that's makin' sure we got somebody to enforce the laws around here. Ophir needs a town marshal, and I figure the best man for the job is Skye Fargo!"

Most of the council members turned to look at Fargo. He returned their gazes steadily and shook his head.

"What?" Boothe said. "What do you mean by that, Fargo?"

"I mean I'm not interested in being the marshal of Ophir or anywhere else," Fargo said.

"I could have told you that," Sprague said to the others. "I made him the same offer last night after we both had a run-in with Walt Drummond over that fella Gratton, and he turned me down flat." Sprague glowered at Fargo.

Judge Boothe shook his head. "Well, I just don't understand. You've done lawman work before, Fargo."

"I was never too fond of it, either," Fargo said. "Circumstances led me into it."

"Circumstances like the ones that brought you here to Ophir?"

Fargo sensed that he wasn't going to win this argument on its merits. These men had their hearts set and their minds made up, and logic didn't necessarily enter into it. But maybe he could divert them.

"What you need to do is make someone else marshal, someone who'll be here permanently," he suggested. "I could stay around for a while, lend a hand when I'm needed, sort of unofficial-like."

"But who else could be our marshal?" one of the men asked.

Fargo nodded toward Patterson. "How about Joe?"

Patterson's eyes widened in surprise. "Me? Who'd make me a lawman? I ain't never wore a badge."

"You know just about everybody in town, don't you?"

"Well, yeah, I reckon."

"And you're on good terms with most of them."

"I 'spose."

"Good enough so that when you talk, they'll listen to you," Fargo said. "That's half the job of keeping the peace right there, just getting people to listen to reason."

"Well, maybe." Patterson was becoming more intrigued with the idea. "I got a livery stable to run, through."

"You could do that and be the marshal, too," Parkhurst said.

Patterson rubbed his chin. "Well, I reckon Dickie could handle most of the work at the stable . . ." He nodded. "By golly, I'll do it! If you boys want me as the town marshal, I'll give it a try." He looked at Fargo. "Don't you go forgettin' that you promised to give me a hand when I need it, though."

"I won't forget," Fargo said with a smile.

Judge Boothe hopped down from the counter with an ease that belied his age and rubbed his hands together. "We got a mayor's race set up and appointed a marshal. I'd say that's a pretty good mornin's work. If there ain't anybody who's got any objections, I declare this meetin' adjourned."

"Good," Sprague said. "I've probably got customers waiting."

Judge Boothe said, "Once this here town gets civilized, you'll have more customers than you can shake a stick at, Sprague."

That was probably right, Fargo thought—and when the day came that Ophir was well and truly civilized, he hoped that he was somewhere else, some place where there was still some wildness in the world.

That afternoon he rode up the valley, following the creek. When he passed the spot where the Conways had been camped the night before, he saw that the wagon was gone. They had moved on in search of their prospecting claim, just as Dinah had said they would.

It took Fargo not quite an hour to find them. They had forded the creek in the wagon, then followed the stream a mile or two farther to where a smaller creek branched off into a side canyon. The narrower stream ran along the base of a rocky, overhanging bluff. On the other side of the creek was a strip of open ground about a hundred yards wide that was bordered with a thick growth of pines. The wagon was stopped beside the creek. As Fargo rode up and reined in, he heard the familiar ringing sound of ax blades biting into tree trunks. Someone was in those pines felling trees.

Dinah must have heard him riding up. She emerged from the wagon, climbing onto the seat and then dropping to the ground. "Skye!" she called. "You came to see us."

Fargo smiled as he swung down from the saddle. "I told you I would. I reckon that's Harry and your pa chopping down trees over yonder?"

"Pa wanted to get to work building a sluice right away." Dinah gestured toward the fast-growing, crystal-clear stream. "He says there's bound to be color in that creek."

Fargo looked at the stream and thought that Conway might be right. There could well be gold dust in there ready to be sluiced out. On his way up here, Fargo had passed more than a dozen other claims, some of them equipped with elaborate sluices and long toms, others nothing more

56

than a man with a battered tin pan standing in the icy
waters of the main creek or its tributary. When he looked
up at the ridges that formed the valley, he saw evidence of
men digging tunnels in them, searching for gold that way.
Here in the Sierra Nevadas, there was no telling what might
make a man rich.

A few minutes later, Frank and Harry Conway came out
of the trees, using a couple of the draft horses from the
wagon team to pull a tree they had chopped down. The
pine was fairly young and once it was sawed up, it would
be enough for several of the legs that the sluice Conway
was planning to build here required. He and Harry would
have to split some of the logs and hew them down into
rough planks to construct the bed. It would be hard,
backbreaking work for a while, Fargo knew, but in the
end it could pay off big if there was enough color in
the stream.

"Mr. Fargo!" Conway called as he led the team of horses
over to the creek. "Good to see you again! What brings
you out here?"

"Curiosity, I reckon. I just wanted to have a look at
your claim."

"What do you think of it?" Conway asked.

Fargo nodded. "Looks like it might turn out to be a good
one. If it's not, you can always move on. That's one of the
good things about living in a big country."

"Reckon there's any bears around here?" Harry asked.

"There sure could be," Fargo replied. "You'd do well to
keep an eye out for them. Sometimes they're attracted to
any food you've got in camp."

"What about Indians?" Dinah asked.

Fargo shook his head. "Not around here. A little farther
north there's some trouble with them from time to time,
but here you ought to be safe." He grinned at Harry. "Except for the bears."

"Aw, you're makin' fun of me," Harry said.

"Just a little," Fargo admitted with a chuckle.

"You'll stay and share our midday meal?" Conway
asked.

Fargo saw the hope on Dinah's face that he would say
yes, so he nodded. "Sure, I'd be proud to."

Conway put his hands on his hips and looked around.

"The first meal in our new home," he said. "Sounds mighty good, don't it?"

Fargo had to agree that it did.

While they ate, Conway pointed out where he intended to build the sluice, and after that, a cabin for the family. There were plenty of trees close at hand. Given time and some hard work, the Conways could have themselves a nice place, Fargo thought. But everything depended on what they found in the creek.

After lunch, Fargo went to help Conway and Harry in the woods, to pay them back for the food he had eaten. He swung one of the axes and felled a couple of pines. Conway did the same. Harry was left to hook chains around the trees and use the horses to drag the logs over to the campsite. The afternoon grew warm, and after a while Fargo paused to take his shirt off. He was stripped to the waist when Dinah came into the trees to bring him a drink of water.

He saw the hunger in her eyes as her gaze roamed over the broad, muscular expanse of his chest. She handed him the dipper of water. He took it and drank and looked at her, and something passed between them, something silent but deep and strong. Fargo felt a liking for Dinah that went far beyond the physical, as enjoyable as that was. She was smart and beautiful and loyal to her family, the sort of young woman who was helping to bring good things to this wild country. Fargo might regret the passing of some of that wildness, but he couldn't regret the fact that Dinah Conway had come to California.

Fargo worked with the ax most of the afternoon, stopping only when it came time to start back to Ophir if he wanted to reach the settlement before dark. As he pulled his shirt on, Dinah suggested, "You could stay and have supper with us, too, Skye."

"No, I'd better be going," Fargo said. "Judge Boothe and the new town council were going to start spreading the word about the election for mayor and Joe Patterson's appointment as marshal. Some people aren't going to like that very much." He thought about Walt Drummond as he spoke. "There could be trouble, and like or not, I suppose I'm the unofficial deputy."

"You be careful," Dinah said as Fargo put on his hat. She touched his arm for a second. Fargo knew she wanted to kiss him—he felt the same way—but with Conway and Harry right there, it wasn't a good idea. He settled for giving Dinah a smile and a nod and walked over to the Ovaro.

Conway strolled after him. The man might have been a greenhorn, but he wasn't blind. In a quiet voice, he said, "I reckon you'll be coming out here to see us again, Mr. Fargo?"

"More than likely," Fargo said.

"Good. You'll always be welcome."

Conway was telling him that he had no objection to him courting Dinah. The man had no idea that things had already gone past the courting stage. Fargo didn't intend to tell him, either. He just nodded, swung up into the saddle, and sent the Ovaro back down the valley toward Ophir.

The sun was well behind the western peaks by the time he got there, but enough rosy light lingered in the sky that he had no trouble staying on the trail. The double doors of Patterson's livery barn were still open. Fargo rode in and found the stableman forking hay down from the loft.

"Howdy, Fargo," Patterson called. "You can just leave your horse. I'll tend to him in a minute."

Fargo swung down from the saddle and left the reins dangling. "Anything happen in town this afternoon?"

Patterson leaned on the pitchfork handle and grinned down at Fargo. "You mean did some folks get a mite upset when they heard that Ophir's got a town council and a marshal and is fixin' to have a mayor? Damn right they did. Walt Drummond especially. O' course, it didn't help that Omar Sprague went over to the Gold Bar and started lambastin' Drummond again." Patterson rubbed his jaw. "I'm goin' to have to have me a talk with Omar. He told Drummond that I'd come and arrest him if anything happened to hurt Omar's business. He shouldn't ought to say things like that. I'm a lawman now. I got to go by the law, not by what some fella says I ought to do."

Fargo nodded. Patterson was beginning to understand one of the burdens of packing a badge—a marshal had to have evidence before he could arrest anyone. Patterson wasn't going to let himself be a blind tool of the town council or let anyone use him and his office to settle personal grudges. That was a good thing, Fargo thought, and he was glad to see that his instincts had been right when he suggested giving the job to Patterson.

"How did Natalie Talmadge react to the news?" Fargo asked.

"I don't reckon she was real happy about it, but she didn't raise a ruckus. She said she'd do her best to operate inside the law, as long as ever'body else in town did the same."

Fargo was glad to hear that, too. He didn't want Natalie getting in trouble with the law.

"Think I'll go on over to the Top-Notch, maybe have some supper there," he told Patterson. "See you later."

Night had settled down over the town while Fargo was talking to the liveryman. Dusk had been short-lived. Now, as Fargo walked toward the Top-Notch, darkness cloaked the alleys between the buildings. Fargo felt a slight tension as he passed the mouths of the narrow lanes. More than once in his eventful career, gunmen waiting in dark alleys had ambushed him.

Tonight, though, Ophir seemed peaceful. He crossed one of the side streets and stepped up onto the boardwalk where the corner entrance to the Top-Notch was located. Music and laughter came from the saloon, beckoning him on with its siren song. Fargo reached for the batwings, intending to thrust them aside.

He stopped short as he saw a flare of light from the corner of his right eye. It was fleeting, there and then gone, but Fargo's keen senses had detected it. His head turned in that direction as he peered toward the far corner of the building. He saw a tiny orange glow, so faint as to be almost undetectable. But as Fargo's eyes narrowed and his forehead creased in a frown, he saw that the light was beginning to grow brighter.

Instinct and experience made him break into a run. He pounded along the side of the building, and as he ran he slipped the Colt from its holster on his hip. His boots slid a little on the dirt as he reached the corner and swung around it in a tight turn. He saw what he'd been afraid he would see—flames beginning to leap up about halfway along the rear wall of the saloon.

Fargo opened his mouth to bellow a warning, but before he could say anything, someone jumped him, tackling him from the side and slamming him to the ground.

5

The Colt slipped out of Fargo's hand when he hit the ground. He sensed as much as heard something coming at his head and twisted away from it. The light from the fire flickered on cold steel as a knife blade jabbed into the dirt next to his ear. He struck upward with a fist and felt a satisfying impact shiver up his forearm as the blow landed against his assailant's jaw.

Fargo rolled toward the man and grabbed his wrist. Fargo's other hand went to the man's elbow. He shoved hard while at the same time yanking on the man's wrist, and he heard a loud *pop!* as the elbow dislocated. The man howled in pain and dropped the knife.

Fargo didn't know if the shout could have been heard inside the Top-Notch over the usual saloon noises. He tried again to yell a warning as he came up on hands and knees, but a second man attacked him with a rush of feet. The sharp toe of a boot drove into Fargo's side and knocked him down, sending him rolling toward the fire.

Fargo felt the heat of the flames against his face. Their glare made it brighter in the alley now. He saw his two opponents, one of them crawling away and cradling his injured arm, the other rushing at Fargo again and swinging some sort of keg. Fargo threw up an arm to block the blow as it fell. The wooden keg smashed against his arm, and he caught the sharp reek of coal oil. That was how the men had started the fire, he realized. They'd poured coal oil along the back wall of the saloon just to make sure the fire got a good hold on the building.

Fargo's left arm was numb from the smashing blow. He rolled out of the way of another kick. The .man loomed over him, a nightmarish figure in the garish, flickering light that might have come from the very flames of Hades. Fargo reached up with his right hand, caught hold of the man's boot, and heaved as hard as he could. The man went over backward with a startled yell.

Spotting his Colt lying in the dirt a couple of yards away, Fargo lunged toward it, his arm outstretched. His fingers closed over the butt of the gun. He rolled over and brought the piece up, thumbing back the hammer as he did so. A gust of night wind caught some of the smoke and blew it in Fargo's face, blinding him for a moment. He coughed as the acrid stuff stung his nose and eyes and throat. His sight cleared just in time for him to see the second man lunging at him, swinging a length of wood he had picked up somewhere in the alley.

That bludgeon would shatter his skull if it hit him. Without hesitation, Fargo fired. His shot caught the man in the shoulder and flung him backward. The makeshift club went spinning off into the darkness.

Another shot blasted. This one came from the first man, the one whose elbow Fargo had dislocated. He had forced himself to his feet and was leaning against the wall, his useless right arm dangling at his side. He was firing with his other hand, and that probably threw his aim off a little as he triggered again. Both slugs whined past Fargo's head. The Colt bucked in Fargo's hand as he returned the fire. His bullets pinned the man to the wall. The man began to slide down toward the ground, leaving dark streaks of blood on the wood behind him.

Fargo's left arm hurt like blazes, and his eyes stung and watered from the smoke. Coughing, he lurched to his feet and looked for the second man, the one he had shot before his partner tried to brain him. The man seemed to have disappeared.

A gun roared in Fargo's ear. He twisted, not sure if he was hit or not, and saw another stab of flame in the darkness as the second man fired at him. Battered and disoriented, Fargo was acting on instinct as much as anything else when he thumbed off a shot. A few yards away, a dark figure doubled over and collapsed.

The flames were roaring now as they climbed up the rear wall of the Top-Notch, but Fargo could barely hear them, still half-deafened as he was by the close report of the gun. Both of his opponents were down, out of the fight. He jammed the Colt back into its holster and looked around for something with which to fight the fire. He spotted a burlap sack in a pile of trash, snatched it up, and began beating at the flames with it.

Suddenly, men were beside him and all around him. He heard them shouting, though it sounded to him as if the yells came from far, far away. Buckets were passed from hand to hand, water sloshing out of the wooden containers. The men closest to the fire threw the water on the flames and handed the empty buckets back. Some of them, like Fargo, found sacks to beat at the flames or even took off their shirts and used them in an attempt to snuff out the blaze.

As the heat grew worse, Fargo stumbled back a step, and someone caught hold of his arm. He looked over into the pale, frightened face of Natalie Talmadge. Her mouth was moving as she shouted something at him, but the only words he caught were "Fargo" and "right."

He nodded, figuring she was asking him if he was all right. He gulped down some air and went back to slapping at the fire with the smoldering sack in his hands. As he did so, he realized that he was using both arms now. The left one ached, but feeling had returned to it and Fargo was glad of that.

Natalie tugged at his arm, and after a moment Fargo allowed her to lead him away from the fire. There were plenty of men fighting the flames now. The alley was full of them, in fact, and they seemed to be bringing the blaze under control. A raging fire was one of the things that frontier folks feared the most. Flames could level an entire town in what seemed like nothing flat.

Hacking and coughing, Fargo leaned on Natalie until they reached the front of the building. Then he put his hands on a hitch rack and leaned forward to cough the last of the smoke out of his lungs. When he straightened, Natalie asked, "Skye, what happened back there?"

His hearing had returned, he noted. Her words were clear to his ears. He said, "Two men started that fire. I came along just as they were doing it and tried to stop them, but I was too late." His voice, hoarse from the smoke he'd breathed in, sounded strange to him.

"I had just caught a whiff of smoke when the shooting started out back," Natalie said. "Why didn't you yell fire?"

Fargo shook his head. "I tried, but those bastards kept jumping me. They wouldn't use their guns because they didn't want to alert anybody to what was going on, so one of them came at me with a knife while the other one tried to stomp my guts out and then bust my head open with a club. Once I'd fired a shot, though, they knew all bets were off, so they went for their own guns and tried to kill me while they had the chance."

"But who were they? Who would do such a thing?" Natalie's face hardened in the light that came from the saloon as she realized the most likely answer to her own question. "Gratton's men," she said. "And I'll bet Walt Drummond gave the orders."

"We don't know that," Fargo pointed out.

"I know all I need to know. Those bastards." She looked up the street toward the Gold Bar. "And there's one of them now."

Fargo looked and saw Drummond's powerful, bald-headed figure standing on the boardwalk in front of the Gold Bar. He was watching the commotion around the Top-Notch. He hadn't come to help fight the fire, though, which was a little unusual. In times of trouble that threatened the entire town, nearly all the citizens turned out to help.

That was evident to Fargo as several familiar, smoke-grimed figures came around the corner of the building. He saw Judge Boothe, Doc Parkhurst, Omar Sprague, and Joe Patterson among the group. Other men were dragging the bodies of the two who had started the fire.

"Fargo!" Boothe said. "What are you doin' here?"

Natalie answered for him, saying, "Skye's the one who first noticed the fire."

Patterson jerked a thumb toward the two dead men and said to Fargo, "Then I reckon you'd be the fella to ask about these carcasses."

"They started the fire," Fargo said, "and then they tried to kill me to keep me from warning anybody. Once the lead started flying, I was a little luckier than they were."

Patterson grunted. "A whole heap luckier, I'd say, seein'

as how you're still alive and they ain't. That was pretty good shootin', Fargo."

"Is the fire out?"

Judge Boothe said, "Yep." He looked at Natalie. "I'm told you're the owner of this here establishment, ma'am?"

"That's right," Natalie said.

"Well, you got considerable damage back there, but nothin' that can't be patched up. Looks to me like you got off light, thanks to Fargo."

"Yes, I know," Natalie said as she looked at Fargo. "And I fully intend to show Mr. Fargo my appreciation."

Fargo saw several of the men grinning at that comment. To change the subject, he gestured toward the corpses and said to Patterson, "Does anybody recognize those two?"

"I don't rightly know. Let's take a look."

The bodies were moved over into the light. Fargo studied their rough, beard-stubbled faces for a long moment, then shook his head. "I don't remember ever seeing them before. They look like typical hardcases."

"They must be Gratton's men," Natalie said.

"I don't recollect 'em, either," Patterson said. " 'Course, Gratton could have some boys ridin' with him that none of us have ever seen."

Fargo had already thought the same thing. He was convinced, though, that these two men had not been part of the gang of toughs that he and the Conways had encountered on the road outside of town a couple of days earlier.

Quite a few people were gathered around. No one admitted knowing the two dead men. The undertaker arrived and enlisted the help of several men to take the bodies along to his place of business. The crowd began to disperse.

Natalie called them back. "Drinks are on the house at the Top-Notch, boys," she said. "That's the least I can do for all of you who helped put out the fire. Without you, I wouldn't even have a saloon now."

With whoops of appreciation, the crowd surged into the saloon. Natalie linked her arm with Fargo's and hung back. She said, "We'll go around the other way. There are some back stairs and a private entrance."

Fargo wasn't going to argue with that. After everything

he had gone through, the idea of braving the bar and its boisterous crowd didn't sound that appealing to him.

The prospect of spending some time alone with Natalie was a lot more intriguing, he decided.

As before when he had walked arm in arm with her, the soft roundness of her breast pressed against him. She led him down the alley on the other side of the building until they came to a narrow set of outside stairs. As they walked up the stairs, their hips brushed together, and Fargo enjoyed the easy intimacy of the contact.

When they reached the landing at the top of the stairs, Natalie produced a key from somewhere inside the tight gown she wore and unlocked the door. It opened into a short, dimly lit hallway with a room on each side. She went to the door on the left and used the same key to unlock it. As she stepped into the dark room, she said to Fargo, "Wait here and I'll get a lamp lit."

Fargo felt a sudden twinge of apprehension as Natalie vanished into the blackness. Somebody could be lurking in there, just waiting to ambush her. Considering everything that was going on in Ophir these days, that didn't seem like such a far-fetched idea to Fargo.

Nothing happened, though, and a moment later a match scraped and flame leaped up from its head. Natalie held the match to the wick of a lamp until it caught, then lowered the glass chimney. The lamp's yellow glow spread, filling all but the corners of the room. Fargo stepped inside and closed the door behind him.

It was a good-sized room and well furnished with a four-poster bed, a dressing table, several armchairs, and a rolltop desk. In one corner, the clawed foot of a bath tub stuck out from behind a screen. A set of moose antlers hung on the wall over the desk, impressive in their width. Natalie saw Fargo looking at the antlers and laughed.

"Those aren't mine," she said. "They were there when I bought the place and moved in. One of the previous owners must have been a hunter, but he didn't take this trophy with him for some reason."

"You don't collect trophies?" Fargo asked with a grin.

"Not that you can hang on the wall," Natalie said.

Fargo chuckled, then winced as he moved his left arm a little, testing it.

"What happened to your arm?"

"One of those men who started the fire tried to break a keg over my head. I took the blow on this arm instead."

Natalie came closer. "You'll have quite a bruise, I imagine. You're lucky the arm wasn't broken. It does still work, doesn't it?"

She was within easy reach. Fargo lifted both arms and put them around her. "Seems to," he said as he brought her tight against him.

Natalie smiled up at him as she put her arms around his neck. Her eyes were heavy-lidded now, and her lips were parted. Fargo brought his mouth down on hers.

Her tongue teased his lips and drew his tongue out into a hot, wet fencing match. Her big, soft breasts pillowed themselves on his chest. Fargo drank in the sweetness of her, reveling in the taste and the heat. The danger he had survived earlier had made all his senses even keener than usual. The fragrance of her hair, of her skin, was maddening.

Thoughts of Dinah Conway flickered across his mind. Fargo was very fond of Dinah, but she had seemed to understand that neither of them had any sort of claim on the other. What had passed between them was exciting and wonderful. Dinah had admitted herself, however, that she wasn't making a present of her innocence to Fargo, and she had no expectations beyond the pleasures they had shared. Fargo had never been the sort to burden himself with false guilt, and he felt none now. He could make love to Natalie Talmadge, if that was what she wanted, with a clear conscience.

Natalie drew back and said, "You smell a little smoky. I was going to have some supper brought up, but would you rather have a bath first?"

Fargo sniffed. The smell of smoke lingered around him. He said, "Maybe a bath would be a good idea."

"I'll tell the cook to start heating some water." She slipped out of his arms and went to the door. "In the meantime, have some brandy." She pointed toward a crystal decanter on the dressing table. Two short, heavy glasses sat beside it. "Pour me one while you're at it."

68

Natalie left the room. Fargo did as she had said and poured brandy for both of them. A short time later, one of the bartenders knocked on the door and came in carrying a big bucket of steaming water. He poured it into the tub and left without even looking at Fargo, who stood there sipping brandy. Fargo wondered how many "guests" had bathed up here in Natalie's room, then put the question out of his mind. It wasn't any of his business.

For the next half hour, men trooped in and out of the room with buckets of hot water. Natalie came in while that was going on and reported to Fargo, "We'll have supper up here in about an hour, Skye. Is that all right?"

"Fine," Fargo told her. "You don't have to treat me like royalty, you know."

She smiled up at him and touched his arm. "Nothing's too good for the man who saved my business."

Fargo didn't point out that he had hardly saved the Top-Notch by himself. Natalie had said that she smelled smoke just before the shooting started. Even if there hadn't been any gunshots, she might have alerted the town to the blaze in time for it to be extinguished. There was no way of knowing.

Fargo didn't intend to turn down the pampering, though. Not when it was coming from a beautiful woman like Natalie.

Finally, when the claw-footed tub was nearly full and wisps of steam were still rising from the water, she tested the temperature with a finger and smiled up at Fargo. "Perfect," she declared. "It's time for you to get out of those clothes, Skye."

"I don't believe in false modesty," he said.

"Good. Neither do I." She turned around so that her back was to him. "Come over here and help me unfasten this dress."

Grinning, Fargo went to her and began unhooking the row of fasteners that went down her back. He bent and kissed the back of her neck just below the hairline. His tongue licked over her skin.

"My, that feels good," Natalie murmured.

When Fargo had all the gown's fasteners undone, he peeled it off her torso and slid it down over her hips. She wore several petticoats over a corset, and he took those off of her as well. Then, still wearing a corset, she turned to face him again. Her ample breasts spilled out of the skimpy garment.

"Now we need to get rid of some of your clothes," she said.

He let her undress him. She didn't stop until he was naked. He was erect, his manhood sticking out long and hard from the thick hair of his groin. Natalie lowered herself to her knees in front of him and put both hands around his shaft. "So beautiful," she whispered as she brought the head to her mouth. Her lips opened and took him in.

Fargo stood there resting his hands lightly on her head as she tongued and licked and sucked the thick pole of male flesh. The heat of her mouth seemed to sear his flesh. She snaked one hand between his legs and cupped him from beneath. Her other hand closed tight around the base of his shaft. She was quite talented at what she was doing, Fargo thought. He stood there enjoying her oral caresses, his hips flexing the least bit each time she sucked on the head of his organ. After a few minutes, she must have sensed that his climax was approaching. She drew back and said, "We don't want to waste this." Getting to her feet, she began unlacing the corset.

Fargo watched in admiration as Natalie peeled away the undergarment. Her breasts, though very full, were firm and bobbed only a little as the corset's support was withdrawn. The nipples were dark pink. Fargo's eyes roamed over the rest of Natalie's body, noting with appreciation the firm thighs and the enticing triangle of dark hair between them. Fargo stepped closer to her and ran his fingers through that hair, feeling the beads of moisture that already clung to the strands.

"I hope you don't mind that I intend to share that bath with you," Natalie said.

"Not at all," Fargo told her. "I was hoping you would."

They moved over to the tub of steaming water, and Natalie held Fargo's hand to balance herself as she stepped in first. "*Ahhh,*" she breathed. "That feels so good."

Fargo waited until she had both feet in the tub and had lowered herself against the far end. Then he stepped in, enjoying the heat of the water. Natalie leaned forward, caught hold of his shaft again, and planted a kiss on the head of it. She licked her lips as she smiled up at Fargo.

He sat down, feeling his stiff muscles begin to ease as the hot water covered them. When he was submerged as far as he could go, the water came up onto his broad chest. Natalie was shorter, so on her the water rose to a point just above her breasts.

Fargo leaned back and stretched out his legs as much as possible, placing them on either side of Natalie. She positioned her legs between Fargo's, and he felt her toes dig into his inner thighs, then move on to his erect organ. She pinned the stiffness between the arches of her feet and then moved them up and down, stroking and caressing. Fargo grew even harder as this underwater play continued.

He reached over and cupped her breasts, using his thumbs to stroke the nipples. Natalie purred like a satisfied cat. She slid closer to Fargo, parting her legs to wrap them around his back as he moved toward her. They came together in the center of the tub, Natalie rising above him in the water and then lowering herself so that his organ was pressed between their bellies. She wriggled, creating a delicious friction that raised the temperature beyond what the steaming water could provide.

They kissed again, tongues dancing and thrusting. Fargo reached around her and slipped a hand between her legs. His middle finger entered her, probing the slickness of her femininity. At the same time, his organ explored the valley between the rounded cheeks of her rump. Natalie broke the kiss, closed her eyes, and began moving her head from side to side in response to the passion that surged through her body. "Oh, yes, Skye, yes!" she panted. "I need you there."

Natalie slid down the thick pole, sheathing him at a deliberate pace that nearly drove Fargo mad. Finally, he was buried completely inside her, and her lips sought his again as they sat there joined in ecstasy.

After a moment Fargo began thrusting up with his hips, driving his shaft in and out of Natalie. She met him thrust for thrust, and as they coupled her arms went around him and held him with fierce strength. Fargo returned the embrace, holding Natalie so closely against him it began to seem to him that they had merged into one being, rather than two.

The passion inside both of them built at a frantic pace, lifting them higher and higher. In a matter of minutes, Fargo couldn't hold back any longer. Natalie was ready, too. In an urgent voice, she whispered into his ear, "Give it to me now, Skye! Give me everything!"

Fargo's climax erupted. Natalie jerked and spasmed in his arms and ground herself against him, straining to bury his shaft as deep inside her as possible and milk the last drop from him. Time had no meaning as the two of them shared the culmination of their lovemaking.

When it was finally over, Natalie's head sagged back and her eyes closed. She seemed to be only half-conscious. Fargo cradled her in his strong arms and kissed her chin, her jaw, the fine line of her throat. Natalie wriggled against him and lifted her arms, stretching.

As she gathered her wits back about her, she rested her hands on his shoulders and smiled into his face. "You really know how to treat a girl, Skye."

"And you know how to make a bath a memorable occasion."

She laughed and reached for some soap that lay on a shelf beside the tub. "Let's get you good and clean."

They spent the next fifteen minutes soaping and washing each other and laughing in pure pleasure as they did so. Fargo ducked under the water, came up, and shook his head like a dog, splashing water and making Natalie laugh even more. By the time they stood up, stepped out of the tub, and began drying each other with large, fluffy towels, Fargo felt one hundred percent better than he had earlier. He knew he would be sore tomorrow from the pounding he had taken behind the Top-Notch, but right now he didn't care.

They had timed things just right. One of the bartenders arrived a few minutes later with a big tray full of food, plates, and glasses. Fargo was dressed in his buckskins by then, and Natalie was wearing a silk dressing gown that clung to the curves of her body in an enticing fashion. The bartender also had a bottle of champagne with him. He started to open it, but Fargo took it from him and said, "I'll take care of that."

The man arched an eyebrow but nodded his agreement. He left the room, closing the door behind him with a soft *click*. Natalie began piling food on plates while Fargo used his thumbs to ease the cork out of the neck of the champagne bottle. It came free with a *pop* and leaped into the air. Fargo caught it.

"I see you've opened bottles of champagne before," Natalie said.

"I'm a man of many talents," Fargo replied with a grin. He filled both glasses and handed one of them to Natalie. She took it and sipped while giving him a sultry look over the top of the glass.

The meal was excellent, especially considering that it had been prepared in a gold-mining boomtown in the middle of the Sierra Nevadas. The food tasted more like it came from a restaurant in San Francisco or St. Louis. When Fargo commented on that, Natalie said, "I hired a new cook a few days ago. He's a Russian, but he's lived all over the world, he says."

Fargo recalled the clerk at the Drake Hotel mentioning a Russian guest. He made a mental note to ask Judge Boothe about the man, since Boothe was sharing a room with him.

After they had eaten, Fargo and Natalie wound up in the four-poster bed, making love again. The second time lacked some of the urgency of the first, but it made up for that with a slow-paced, overwhelming sensuousness. When they had both climaxed again, Natalie snuggled down in the pillows and covers and murmured, "I think I'll sleep for a week."

Fargo laughed and said, "You do that." He bent over and kissed her cheek. She smiled, but didn't open her eyes.

He slipped out of bed and got dressed. Then he left the room and went down the rear stairs they had used earlier, making sure that the doors were locked behind him.

The night air was cool. Fargo walked around the saloon to check on the damage from the fire. Black, sooty smudges on the wall showed how high the flames had climbed. The wall itself was still structurally sound, however. Fargo knew some of the planks would have to be replaced, and maybe some of the studs inside the wall, too, but a good carpenter could have the job finished in a few days without too much trouble or expense.

Fargo frowned in the darkness as he thought about the situation. He walked back to the main street and paused there on the boardwalk. The evening's festivities were still in full swing inside the saloon. The same could be said of the Gold Bar in the next block. Fargo found his long strides carrying him in that direction.

He pushed through the batwings into Drummond's place and paused to look around. As usual, it was crowded but not quite as busy as the Top-Notch. Fargo's eyes were drawn across the room toward a table in the rear. Two men sat there, both of them burly and powerful-looking. Fargo recognized them.

Drummond was the first to notice Fargo standing there watching him. The bald-headed saloonkeeper raised a hand, signaling for his companion to stop talking. Gratton, who sat with his back turned halfway to the rest of the room, saw the direction Drummond was looking and swiveled his head on his bull neck to look the same way. When he saw Fargo, his upper lip drew back in an angry grimace. He started to get to his feet, but Drummond put out a hand and stopped him.

So Drummond and Gratton were having a parley, Fargo thought as he started across the room toward the table where the two men sat. That was interesting. It didn't prove anything except that they knew each other, but it was still interesting.

Drummond put a smile on his face as Fargo came up to the table. "Evening," he said. His voice held a hint of mockery as he went on, "I think you two boys know each other."

"I know this son of a bitch, all right," Gratton said. "He's the skunk who killed poor Dunkle."

"Dunkle went for his gun first," Fargo said. "After you'd taken a beating."

Gratton's face still bore the marks of that fight. His bruised features twisted, and Fargo could feel the rage radiating from the man. Again Gratton started up out of his chair, but he stopped himself this time. "What the hell," he muttered. "It's not worth it." He stared at Fargo. "But one of these days, mister, you and me are going to settle things between us."

"I'm looking forward to it," Fargo said.

This time Gratton did shove his chair back and stand up, but there was no menace in the action. He threw another cold glare at Fargo, then turned and walked off, stalking out of the Gold Bar. Several nervous looks followed him as he slapped the batwings aside and disappeared into the night. Gratton had plenty of people in Ophir afraid of him, but not all. Not by any means.

"What do you want, Fargo?" Drummond asked. "How about a drink?"

Fargo shook his head. "I don't think so."

Drummond gave a humorless bark of laughter. "Now that you've run off one of my paying customers, don't you think you ought to take his place?"

"Gratton was a paying customer?"

"Of course."

"There are no drinks on the table," Fargo pointed out.

"That's because they hadn't been brought over yet." Drummond lifted a finger in a signal to the bartender. "Have one on me, Fargo."

Fargo hesitated, then pulled out a chair and sat down. "All right."

The bartender brought over two glasses and a bottle. Fargo watched closely as the drinks were poured. Nothing was in the glass that the bartender shoved over in front of him except whiskey. He had thought that Drummond might try to slip him something.

Drummond picked up his glass. "To resolving misunderstandings," he said.

"I'm not sure what you mean by that."

"You think I'm behind all the trouble around here. Hell, you probably even think I had something to do with the fire that broke out behind Natalie Talmadge's place this evening."

"The thought crossed my mind," Fargo said.

Drummond tossed back his drink when it became obvious Fargo wasn't going to return his unorthodox toast. "I don't know a thing about it," he said as he lowered the empty glass to the table. "Natalie's problems don't have anything to do with me."

"It looked to me when I came in like Gratton was reporting to you."

Drummond's fingers tightened on the glass. "Gratton was trying to convince me to hire him," he said. "He told me he could see to it that I was top dog around here. I told him as far as I'm concerned, I already am. And I was about ready to tell him to go to hell when you came up, Fargo. Maybe I should just tell you that instead."

"Maybe you should." Fargo pushed his glass away with the drink untouched. He stood up and dropped a coin on the table. The gesture made Drummond turn pale with anger. "I told you before I don't want Natalie to have any more trouble. If you had anything to do with that fire, I'll find out about it, and I'll see you behind bars, Drummond."

"You've got it wrong," Drummond said again, his voice tight. "But if you don't believe me, you really can go to hell, Fargo. And start by getting out of my saloon."

"Gladly," Fargo turned and walked out. The skin on his back crawled a little as he did so. He knew he was making a target of himself. But nothing happened. He stepped outside onto the boardwalk.

Pausing to take a deep breath, Fargo brought his own anger under control. Seeing Drummond and Gratton together had just about convinced him that Natalie was right about the owner of the Gold Bar.

And yet, Drummond had sounded sincere when he explained what Gratton was doing there. It was just possible, Fargo thought, that the big saloonkeeper was telling the truth. But if that was the case, then there was more going on here in Ophir than it looked like. There were undercurrents that Fargo had not yet plumbed.

He was turning all that over in his mind as he started toward Patterson's livery stable. Once again it had been a long day and he was ready to turn in for the night. He knew he wouldn't fall asleep for a while, though. His brain would be too busy considering all the possibilities of who could be responsible for the trouble in Ophir. . . .

He was so busy concentrating on the problems of the boomtown that he didn't realize anyone was waiting for him until flame lanced out of the night and a bullet whipped past his ear.

6

Fargo flung himself toward the street, away from the bright wink of the muzzle flash. He went off the low boardwalk, landed in the dirt of the street, and rolled over. His hand slapped at the butt of his gun and palmed out the Colt. The ambusher fired again, and this time the bullet came close enough to Fargo to kick dust and grit into his eyes. Half-blinded, he fired back anyway, letting his instincts aim the shots. He thumbed off three rounds as fast as he could, then rolled again and surged to his feet.

Down the block, men were shouting in alarm and yelling questions as they spilled out of the saloons and gambling dens that lined the street. Fargo ignored them and focused his attention on the spot the shots had come from. He was quite near the livery stable, and as best he could determine, the gunfire had originated there.

Fargo broke into a run, heading for the stable. Nobody shot at him. Though he hadn't heard any footsteps, he suspected the bushwhacker had fled into the night.

As Fargo came closer to the barn, he saw that one of the big double doors in the front was open a couple of feet. That was unusual. Joe Patterson always locked up after dark. Fargo was convinced now that the shots had come from inside the livery stable. When he reached the closed door, he flattened his back against it and listened for a moment, searching with his keen hearing for any sounds that might indicate lurking danger. Instead he heard only a low groan.

Crouching low with the Colt held in front of him ready for instant use, Fargo ducked through the opening into the barn. All the lamps were out, leaving the place in stygian darkness. Fargo dropped down to his knee and remained there, stock-still, as he listened again. Another groan came to his ears, but that was all.

"Joe?" he called. "Joe, are you in here?"

The voice that replied was weak and confused. "F-Fargo? Is that you?"

Fargo stood up, still wary. "Take it easy, Joe," he said. "I'll have a light in a minute."

Several horses were moving around in their stalls, spooked by the gunfire. Fargo recognized the Ovaro's whicker as the big black-and-white stallion called out to him. Relying on his excellent memory, Fargo made his way along the aisle in the center of the barn to the door of the tack room. He put out his free hand and found the lantern hanging there on a nail.

One-handed, he fumbled out a match and struck it, then lit the lantern. A yellow glow washed out from it and formed a circle of light. Joe Patterson lay at the edge of that circle on the hard-packed floor of the barn. Blood made a dark smudge on his brow as he lifted his head to look at Fargo.

"Wh-what the hell happened?" Patterson asked.

Fargo holstered his Colt, convinced at last that the bush-whacker was gone. He went over to Patterson and leaned down to grasp the liveryman's arm. As he helped Patterson to his feet, he said, "You tell me. Somebody waiting in here tried to kill me a few minutes ago."

A few of the townspeople who were braver than their fellows appeared in the doorway of the stable in time to hear Fargo's words. Startled exclamations came from them, and the news began to make its way along the street that Fargo had been ambushed and nearly killed.

Patterson pulled a rag from his pocket and held it to the bleeding gash on his forehead. "I was just about to lock up for the night," he said. "It was a mite later than usual when I got around to it. Somebody must've slipped in here while I was in the back. I heard somebody behind me and started to turn around, and whoever it was clouted me with a pistol. Must've been a pistol. I ain't never been hit that hard in my life."

Fargo nodded. The injury to Patterson's forehead was

consistent with being pistol-whipped. He said, "Did you get a look at whoever it was?"

Patterson shook his head and winced at the fresh pain that stabbed through his skull. "Nope, it was too dark in here. I got turned around just far enough so's he could hit me in the front of the head. All I saw before that was a shadow. It was pretty good-sized, though, so I know it was a man."

Fargo's face was grim as he thought about what Patterson had just told him and remembered the run-in with Gratton at the Gold Bar. After leaving Drummond's place, Gratton would have had plenty of time to come over here, knock out Patterson, and wait for Fargo to show up. Gratton had warned Fargo that he intended to settle the score between them. Somehow, a bushwhacking didn't seem to Fargo like the way Gratton would go about it, but he couldn't say for certain. Gratton could have decided to take the easy way out and tried an ambush.

"I'm sorry, Joe," Fargo said. "The bastard who walloped you was really after me. You just happened to be in his way."

"Yeah, I reckon you're right. You weren't hit, were you?"

Fargo shook his head. "No, his aim wasn't quite good enough. And he took off for the tall and uncut when I started shooting back at him. I suppose he wanted to wait for another time, when the odds were on his side again."

One of the bystanders must have sent for Dr. Parkhurst, because the medic showed up then, pushing his way through the crowd at the entrance of the livery stable. Parkhurst came up to Patterson and said, "Let's see that head of yours, Joe."

Patterson grinned as he lowered the rag, exposing the gash on his forehead. "It ain't nothin' to worry about, Doc. It'd take more'n a six-shooter to dent this noggin of mine."

"Maybe so, but I'd like to clean up that wound and see if it needs any stitches. Let's go in your office." Parkhurst glanced at Fargo. "Are you all right?"

"I'm fine, Doc. You go tend to Joe."

While Parkhurst and Patterson went into the office,

Fargo turned to the men at the door and asked if any of them had seen anyone fleeing from the vicinity of the livery barn. All he got back were shakes of the head and muttered negatives. Fargo tended to believe them, but it was possible at least one of them had seen the bushwhacker and recognized him as Gratton. A witness could be too frightened of the big renegade to admit to what he had seen.

Fargo heard a yelp of pain from the office, and when he looked in, he saw Parkhurst putting the finishing touches on a couple of stitches in Patterson's forehead. "That should do it," the doctor said as he snipped off the suture. "I'll put a bandage over the wound to keep it clean. The scar shouldn't be too bad, Joe."

"I ain't worried about a scar or two. I got plenty of 'em already." Patterson's hands clenched into fists. "I'd like to get hold of the son of a buck who hit me, though. I'd teach him a thing or two. Shoot, he assaulted an officer of the law!"

"That's right," Fargo agreed. "You're the marshal of Ophir now, Joe. If we can identify whoever it was, you can hold him on that charge as well as trying to shoot me."

"I'll do it, too. You know, Fargo, it seems to me it's time to start thinkin' about buildin' a jail here."

"That's a good idea. Why don't you take it up with Judge Boothe?"

"I sure will, first thing tomorrow."

Parkhurst closed and fastened his medical bag after he'd tied a square bandage over Patterson's injury. "I'm not needed here anymore," he said. "I'm going to go get some sleep while I've got the chance."

"Sounds like a good idea," Fargo said. He shooed away the few curious onlookers who hadn't already left the barn, waved good night to Parkhurst, and turned back to the ladder leading to the loft. Before climbing up, he asked Patterson, "You going to be all right, Joe?"

"Sure. But I'll be better when I catch whoever done this."

Fargo hoped that came about. He didn't like being shot at out of the dark—or any other way.

*   *   *

To Fargo's surprise, things quieted down in Ophir for a few days after that. He supposed it was the law of averages. Hell couldn't keep popping up all the time.

There were too many tracks and footprints in Joe Patterson's barn for Fargo to be able to tell which set of prints belonged to the bushwhacker. With no trail to follow, Fargo had to admit that the man had made a clean getaway, though doing so was a bitter pill to swallow. Still, he didn't brood over the situation. That wasn't his nature. Instead he spent quite a bit of time at the Top-Notch, enjoying the company of Natalie Talmadge. The nights in her bed were most enjoyable, in fact.

The campaign for mayor got underway, although it looked to Fargo as if both Doc Parkhurst and Omar Sprague were running like they were trying to get the other candidate elected. Both men made speeches at a public rally praising their opponent. Neither man was much of a public speaker. Of the two, Sprague was the more polished. Fargo sensed that Parkhurst was better liked among the townspeople though. He didn't know a lot about politics, and didn't want to know any more than he had to, but he watched the opening steps of the campaign with some interest.

There was also quite a bit of talk in town about the jail that Joe Patterson was going to build. With Judge Boothe's backing, Patterson recruited a couple of prospectors who had given up on their claims to fell some trees and start putting up a sturdy log building. Patterson had what Fargo thought was a good idea about how to construct the jail.

"There'll just be one door," Patterson explained to Fargo, "and that'll be in the roof. The building will be flat on top. Prisoners will have to climb up a ladder to get to the roof, then down another ladder to get into the cell. Then I'll pull that ladder up, and they won't have any way to get out. I don't figure on havin' any prisoners escapin'."

Until the jail was ready, Patterson planned to lock up anybody who needed locking up in his tack room. So far, though, he had made no arrests. Judge Boothe and the newly appointed town council had spread the word about Patterson being named marshal, and Boothe had announced as well that he would begin holding court in Omar Sprague's emporium as soon as a session was warranted. With all that going on, it was no wonder that Ophir had become more law-abiding all of a sudden, Fargo thought. Nobody wanted to be the first to test the newly established justice system.

But it would come sooner or later, Fargo knew. No boomtown could stay quiet and peaceful forever.

He was walking down the street one day when he spotted a familiar wagon parked in front of Sprague's emporium. It belonged to Frank Conway, and as Fargo turned his steps in that direction, Conway himself emerged from the store, followed by the apron-clad Omar Sprague.

"My clerks will get that order loaded up for you right away, Mr. Conway," Sprague was saying. "Anything else I can do for you?"

"No, I think that's all," Conway replied. He noticed Fargo approaching and lifted a hand in greeting. "Mr. Fargo! I was hoping we'd run into you when we came into town today."

Fargo shook hands with Conway and said, "It's good to see you again, Frank. Where are Dinah and Harry?"

"Dinah's still inside the store, looking at geegaws." Conway glanced around. "I don't know where Harry's gotten off to, but he's around town somewhere."

Fargo nodded. "I'll step inside and say hello to Dinah."

"I'm sure she'd like that." Conway hesitated for a second, then said, "I sort of expected to see you visiting out at our claim again before now."

"I've been busy here in town," Fargo said.

"Sure, I can understand that. You're welcome any time, though."

Fargo wasn't sure what to say to that. He knew that Conway had an eye on him as a possible husband for his daughter, and Fargo knew as well that such a match was not going to happen. He wasn't ready to settle down in one place, with one woman, no matter how sweet and smart and pretty she was—and Dinah Conway fit that description in spades. Still, he couldn't deny that he wanted to see her again. Even as distracted as he'd been by Natalie Talmadge, he found himself missing Dinah.

"I'll be along," Fargo said, keeping his response to Conway vague. He turned toward the door of the emporium and went inside.

It was dim and cool in the store, but despite the shadows, Dinah Conway's honey-blond hair seemed to shine with a light of its own. Fargo had no trouble finding her. Hearing his boots on the planks of the floor as he approached, she turned, and her face lit up with a smile as she recognized him. "Skye!" she said. "I was hoping we'd see you."

"That's what your father said. How are things out at the claim?"

"Wonderful. We have the sluice built, and we've even found a little gold dust already. Pa says it's good color." Dinah glanced around the store. She and Fargo were alone in this aisle, and the clerks were busy at the long counter in the rear of the building. She stepped closer to Fargo and put a hand on his arm, saying in a half-whisper, "I've missed you so much, Skye. I think all the time about what happened up there in the loft. . . ."

She stopped talking and came up on her toes to give him a quick kiss on the mouth. Their lips were pressed together only for a second, but in that time Fargo tasted the desire in Dinah. She wanted to be with him again, and he found himself wanting that, too.

"I'll come see you," he murmured as he rested his hands on her shoulders for a moment.

"You'd better. And come soon. What about tomorrow?"

Fargo didn't see any reason why he couldn't ride up to the Conway claim the next day. He nodded. "I'll be there."

Heavy footsteps announced that Conway and Sprague had entered the store again. Sprague shook hands with Conway and said, "Thanks for the business."

"You're sure you don't mind carrying part of the debt for a while?" Conway said. "I reckon I'll have it paid off by fall."

Sprague waved off the question. "I pride myself on being a good judge of character, and I think you're a good risk, Conway."

Conway looked over at Fargo and Dinah, who weren't standing quite so close together now. "Ready to go, Dinah?" he asked.

"Yes, Pa." She shot a glance at Fargo that said she would miss him until the next time she saw him.

Dinah went to join her father. Fargo trailed along behind her. As they all came out onto the long, raised porch in front of the emporium, Conway said, "Now if we can just find that blasted brother of yours. Harry's got off somewhere, and I don't have any idea where."

"I'll take a look around town for him," Fargo offered. "I know most of the businesses now. There are only so many places he can be."

"Look in the saloons," Dinah suggested. "Or any other place there are painted women."

Conway frowned. "Dinah, you shouldn't talk that way about your brother. You shouldn't be talking about painted women at all."

"Harry's sixteen years old, Pa. That's about all he's interested in right now."

"I don't care, it's no subject for a decent young woman to discuss."

Dinah glanced at Fargo again, and mischief sparkled in her eyes. He knew she was thinking again about how they had romped in the loft at the livery stable. He looked down at the ground, cleared his throat, and said, "I'll check the saloons, Frank. Maybe you should look some of the other places."

"All right," Conway said with a nod. "Dinah, you stay here with the wagon."

"Yes, Pa."

Fargo could tell that she was still laughing inside as he walked off.

He crossed the street and started working his way along it, looking in at each of the saloons on that side. He didn't see any sign of Harry Conway. When he came to the Top-Notch and paused just inside the batwings, a couple of the bartenders waved at him. They all knew Fargo now. He was a familiar sight in the saloon. He looked around for Natalie, didn't see her, and decided that she was upstairs either sleeping or working on the saloon's bookkeeping. Harry wasn't there, either, so Fargo gave the bartenders a casual wave and stepped out onto the boardwalk again.

As he approached Drummond's Gold Bar, he heard a

sudden burst of angry voices from inside. Fargo frowned. Trouble in Drummond's place was Drummond's worry, not his. On the other hand, Fargo reminded himself, he was serving as an unofficial deputy here in Ophir. If a brawl was about to break out, he ought to see if he could do anything to put a stop to it before it got started.

His pace quickened as he approached the entrance of the saloon. Someone was still shouting inside. Just before Fargo reached the batwings, they flew open and a man came tumbling backward across the boardwalk, moving quickly. He tripped on his own boots and would have gone sprawling if Fargo hadn't jumped forward to catch hold of his arm and steady him. To his surprise, he found himself holding Harry Conway, and the face that the youngster turned toward him was stained with blood that welled from his nose. Harry's upper lip was swelling, too. Fargo recognized the signs of somebody who had just been punched hard in the face.

"Mr. Fargo!" Harry exclaimed in surprise, his voice thick because of the swelling lip.

Someone slapped the batwings aside and said, "Hey, kid! I'm not finished with you!"

Fargo looked over and saw the lean, well-dressed figure of Tom Harlin, the gambler. He was a little surprised because Harlin hadn't struck him as the sort to be brawling, but after all, Harry Conway was little more than a boy. Harlin could have thought it was safe to push him around and knock him through the entrance of the Gold Bar.

If that was the case, Harlin was about to find out he was wrong.

"You're finished with him, all right," Fargo said.

Harlin glared at him. "Who the devil are—No, wait, I know you now. You're the one who came to town with that two-bit judge."

Fargo smiled, but the expression held little genuine humor. "I wouldn't let Judge Boothe hear you call him that."

"I'm not scared of that old fossil." Harlin wasn't drunk, but he had been drinking. He pointed a finger at Harry. "I'm not scared of that kid, either. He needs to be taught a lesson."

Fargo looked at Harry. "What did you do?"

"Nothing, Mr. Fargo, I swear!"

Harlin snorted. "Nothing?" He gestured at a wet spot on his coat. "The little bastard spilled a drink on me because he was too busy ogling the girls to pay attention to what he was doing."

Fargo sniffed. Harry smelled a little like whiskey, all right. He said, "Your pa's not going to be happy about this."

Harry looked miserable. "I'm sorry, Mr. Fargo. I just wanted to see what it was like in a saloon. I've heard so much about them—"

"I don't care about any of that," Harlin cut in. "I want him to pay for what he did to my coat."

"He doesn't have any money," Fargo said.

"Then he can pay by taking a beating."

"I don't think so."

Harlin tensed. He didn't like being challenged this way, and Fargo could see that there was no fear in the gambler's eyes. Harlin had confidence in his ability to get the derringer out of his sleeve and get a shot off before anyone who might be facing him. And Harlin *was* fast. Fargo knew that. He also knew that if it came down to it, he was the faster of the two, and could kill the gambler.

Walt Drummond suddenly appeared behind Harlin and said over his shoulder, "What's going on here?"

"Just trying to teach this damned young pup some manners, Walt," Harlin replied. "He spilled a drink on me."

"Wouldn't be the first drink spilled on you," Drummond said. "I've seen you do it yourself, Tom. Go on back in and tend to your games."

"But, Walt—"

"Do it," Drummond said.

With an evil, resentful gleam in his eyes as he cast one last glance at Fargo and Harry, Harlin turned and went back into the Gold Bar. Drummond stepped aside to let him pass. Facing Fargo, the saloonkeeper said, "You'd better be careful. Tom's the touchy sort."

"Is he the back-shooting sort?"

Drummond chuckled. "I don't think so, but I wouldn't bet my life on it."

"I don't intend to." Fargo paused, then said, "Thanks for stepping in, Drummond."

The burly saloonkeeper shrugged his broad shoulders. "I don't want any gunplay right outside my place. It's bad for business, especially in broad daylight like this. Besides, if you and Tom had drawn on each other, you might have killed him, and I'd lose a good dealer who makes a lot of money for the house. Or he would have killed you and then more than likely turned his gun on the sprout here." Drummond shook his head. "Can't have an employee killing kids. That gives the place a bad name, too."

"I'm not a kid," Harry protested.

"Well, you're not full-grown, either," Drummond sneered. He considered for a second, then went on, "Come back and see me when you are, though. You've got sand. If you've got any brains to go with it, I might be able to use you."

"Forget it," Harry said. "My pa and I are gold miners."

"Good luck to you, then. But don't forget what I said." Drummond looked at Fargo. "Seen Gratton lately?"

"No. He must be lying low. But you'd know that better than I would."

Drummond just shook his head at Fargo's comment. "Still don't believe me, eh? Well, I'm tired of trying to convince you, Fargo." He turned and pushed his way back into the saloon. The batwings looked small as they flapped closed behind his massive form.

"You'd better think twice before you sneak off to that place again," Fargo told Harry. "Come on, let's find your pa."

When they got back to the wagon parked in front of the emporium, they found Dinah waiting for them with an anxious expression on her face. "I saw something going on up there outside that saloon," she said. "That's where you went, isn't it, Harry?"

"Yes, but that's not any business of yours," Harry muttered, his eyes downcast.

"It's my business if you go off and get yourself in trouble! You could have been beaten up, or shot, or . . . or . . . ."

"Where's your father?" Fargo asked.

"He's checking the livery stables and the blacksmith and the other businesses where they don't sell whiskey and hussies."

"Damn it, Dinah, you don't have any right to scold me!"

Harry burst out. "You're a girl. You don't know what it's like to be a fella."

"Maybe not, but I know—well, just never you mind what I know. Get in the wagon, Harry."

Fargo looked away to hide the grin that stretched across his face. Brothers and sisters were just naturally quarrelsome, he supposed, like cats and dogs.

Harry climbed into the back of the wagon, still grumbling, and a few minutes later when Frank Conway came back down the street, Dinah said, "Skye found Harry, Pa. He's in the back now."

"Good. I'm ready to head out to the claim. I don't like leaving it unprotected for too long." Conway looked at Fargo. "Found him in a saloon, did you?"

"Actually, he was on the boardwalk right outside of the Gold Bar," Fargo said. That was the truth. As for the rest of it, he would let the Conways hash that out. It was family business and none of his.

"Don't forget you're coming to see us tomorrow," Dinah said.

Fargo touched a finger to the brim of his hat. "I'm not likely to let something like that slip my mind," he said.

He stood there in front of the emporium and watched the wagon roll away along the street. Omar Sprague came out of the store and stood beside him. "Seems like a fine family," the merchant commented.

"That they are," Fargo agreed.

"Conway was telling me he's got himself a good claim, too. Maybe he's found his fortune."

"Could be," Fargo said. To his way of thinking, Frank Conway already had a fortune, in the form of two fine youngsters like Dinah and Harry. But maybe that was just the loner in him talking, he mused. He'd had his own chances for a family, and every time he had ridden away to follow new trails. That was the way of the world, he told himself. Some men stayed, and others rode on.

Skye Fargo was and likely always would be a trailsman, riding on was his way of life.

The next day, he followed the creek up the valley to the smaller stream and then swung the Ovaro alongside it for the stretch to the Conway claim. It was late in the morning,

Fargo having timed his departure from Ophir so that he would arrive at the claim around the middle of the day. He suspected that Dinah would have a good lunch ready by the time he got there.

The curl of smoke that rose in the air ahead of him tended to confirm that guess. There wasn't much smoke, not enough to be alarming, but rather just enough to be coming from a cooking fire.

A few minutes later, Fargo came within sight of the claim. The long sluice box sat the edge of the stream under the overhanging bluff. Frank Conway stood in the water beside the box, shoveling gravel from the streambed into it. Harry used a bucket to dump water from the creek into the sluice. It ran down the inclined slope of the apparatus, carrying away the dirt and lighter pebbles among the gravel. Small pieces of wood known as riffle bars were lined up crossways on the bottom of the sluice. They caught the heavier debris that was not washed away by the water. If a man was lucky, he found flakes of gold dust, maybe even small nuggets, among that debris. The more gold, the better a claim's "color."

On the open ground some twenty yards from the creek, Fargo saw the beginnings of a cabin's foundation. The Conways had put in some work on a permanent place to live. Most of the hours in the day would be devoted to working the claim, but when winter came they would need a better shelter than the wagon. Frank Conway knew this and was trying to accomplish both goals.

In the meantime, Dinah was cooking over an open fire. As Fargo rode closer to the claim, she straightened from the pot she had been stirring. The big black iron pot was suspended over the flames by a rod that ran between two y-shaped stakes that had been hammered into the ground. It was a primitive but effective way of preparing meals. Some of the best stew Fargo had ever eaten had come from just such a cooking arrangement. As he came closer now, a delicious aroma drifted to his nose. He looked forward to yet another good meal.

Dinah waved at him. So did Harry. As Fargo rode up to the wagon and brought the Ovaro to a halt, Harry splashed out of the stream and started toward him. Frank Conway remained where he was, leaning on his shovel and looking down into the sluice box as the water did its work.

"Hello, Skye," Dinah said as Fargo swung down from the saddle. "I was hoping nothing would happen to keep you from riding out here today."

"The town's quiet this morning," Fargo replied. He looped the Ovaro's reins around the brake lever on the wagon. With a smile, he went on, "Whatever you've got cooking there, it smells mighty good."

Dinah flushed with pleasure at the compliment. "It's just rabbit stew."

"Nothing wrong with that."

"I've got biscuits already cooked to go with it."

"Even better," Fargo told her with a grin.

Harry came up to the camp, swinging the bucket in his right hand. "Howdy, Mr. Fargo," he said. "Pa said for me and Dinah to make you welcome, that he'd be along as soon as that last bucketful of water runs through the sluice box."

"Any color this morning?" Fargo asked.

"A little. Some days are better than others. Pa says that overall the claim is working out just fine, though."

Fargo nodded. He would discuss the situation with Conway while he was here and try to determine if the man's estimate of the claim's value was accurate or if Conway was just being optimistic. Fargo was no expert when it came to prospecting, but he knew a fair amount from spending time in the Sierra Nevadas. He hoped that Conway was right. This was a pleasant place, and it wasn't too far from town. A man could do a lot worse—and plenty had.

Harry's nose and mouth were bruised and swollen from the punch he'd received the day before. Fargo said, "I reckon you probably had a headache this morning."

Harry's face turned red with embarrassment. "You didn't have to come fight my battles for me, Mr. Fargo," he said. "Not that I don't appreciate what you did to help me. I do. But I could've handled that gambler."

Fargo debated for a second between sparing Harry's feelings and telling him something that might serve him in good stead later. He decided the truth might be better, so he said, "Harry, Tom Harlin would have either killed you or at least hurt you quite a bit. He's lived a long time in a violent world, and he knows how to take care of himself. You want to walk careful around that sort of man until you've been out here on the frontier longer."

"I know he's a gunman. That's why I'm not going into Ophir again without this." Harry pulled aside his shirt to reveal the butt of a small pistol tucked behind his belt.

"Harry!" Dinah exclaimed. "That's Pa's old gun. What are you doing carrying it?"

"A man's got to be able to protect himself," Harry said, his voice stubborn. "Mr. Fargo just said so. Besides, *he* carries a gun—two of 'em, in fact, and that big ol' knife—and you think he hung the damn moon!" Harry glanced at Fargo. "No offense, sir."

"None taken," Fargo said. "Your sister has a point, though. You start toting iron before you know how to use it, and you're just asking for trouble."

"I know how to use it," Harry insisted. "I've practiced."

"Once or twice," Dinah said. "And that was just shooting at tin cans. Shooting at a man is a lot different, isn't it, Skye?"

"Dinah's right, Harry," Fargo said. He had a feeling the words weren't going to do any good, though.

"Well, I don't care. I'll be damned if I'll let anybody push me around anymore without fighting back."

Dinah looked at Fargo as if she were pleading with him to talk some sense into Harry's head. He didn't say anything. There came a point in a young man's life when he had to learn his lessons for himself, harsh though they might be. Fargo had a feeling that Harry Conway was fast approaching the point, if indeed he wasn't already there. But he resolved to himself that he would keep a close eye on Harry the next time the youngster came into Ophir. When he got a chance, he would tell that to Dinah in private. Maybe it would ease her mind a little.

Harry walked toward the woods, muttering to himself. Dinah started to go after him, but Fargo motioned for her to wait. Harry needed a little time to himself to cool off.

Fargo turned toward the stream. He saw Frank Conway setting the shovel aside and knew the man was about to join them at the wagon. Conway stepped around the sluice box, then stopped short and looked up toward the top of the bluff with a frown on his face.

Fargo heard the rattle of stones falling and glanced up as well. What he saw made him shout in alarm. "Frank! Get away from there!" Fargo broke into a run toward the stream.

Conway tried to run, too, but he was too late. A huge mass of broken rock slid down the face of the bluff. He screamed as the avalanche caught him, smashing down around him and hiding him in a cloud of dust and falling rock.

7

Fargo jerked back as the dust cloud rolled into his face and blinded him. Dinah screamed, "Pa! Pa," and tried to run past him toward the avalanche. Fargo grabbed her and held her back, keeping his arms tightly around her waist. The rumbling that had accompanied the falling rocks was dying away now, telling Fargo that the slide had stopped for the most part. But there could still be danger. The last rock to fall could kill a person just as dead as the first one.

There was a bitter taste in Fargo's mouth, and it didn't come from the dust and grit he had swallowed. It came from the knowledge that Frank Conway had to be dead. No one could have survived that slide. Even though it had been small as avalanches go, several tons of rock had fallen off the bluff and landed right on top of Conway.

"Pa!" Harry shouted. Fargo turned his head to look and saw the young man racing toward the stream. Dinah was still sobbing and struggling to get out of his grip. He couldn't let go of her to stop Harry. The youngster would have to take his chances. The dust was beginning to settle, though, and Fargo hadn't heard any rocks fall for several moments. The slide was probably over.

Fargo picked up Dinah so that her feet were kicking in the air. He carried her over to the wagon and put her down. Her face was twisted with grief and wet with tears. "Dinah, listen to me!" he said. He hated to speak to her in such a harsh voice, but he knew he had to get through to her. "Stay here! It's dangerous over there by the bluff. Harry and I will see about your father."

"P-Pa! Oh, my God! All those rocks! Wh-where did they come from?"

Fargo wondered that himself, but there would be time

94

later to worry about that. Although he figured it was impossible for Frank Conway to have lived through this catastrophe, miracles were known to happen from time to time. He had to be absolutely certain there was no hope for Conway.

He put his hands on Dinah's shoulders and squeezed hard. "Dinah, are you listening to me? You have to promise me that you'll stay over here where you're safe."

As more tears rolled down her cheeks, she managed to jerk her head in a nod. "G-go help him, Skye," she choked out. "Help Harry."

"That's just what I intend to do."

Confident now that Dinah would stay out of harm's way, Fargo let go of her and turned toward the stream. The dust had settled enough so that he could see the big pile of rocks that formed a crude dam across the stream. The avalanche had crushed the sluice, too. Fargo could see the far end of the long wooden trough, but that was all.

Harry was already among the rocks, tearing at them, picking up the ones he could and tossing them aside. His motions were frantic, hysterical. Fargo hurried toward him. He clambered onto the pile of rocks next to Harry and without saying anything joined him in clearing away the debris.

It took them twenty minutes of hard work, and Fargo's forehead was beaded with sweat before they found Frank Conway's body. Harry uncovered an arm and let out a groan. He started tearing at the remaining chunks of rock even harder and faster. Fargo joined him, and they followed the arm up to the shoulder. Fargo saw how Conway's sleeve was sodden with blood and he caught hold of Harry's arm before Harry could uncover his father's face.

"Maybe you'd better go back over there to the wagon with your sister," he suggested.

"Damn it, no! Pa may be . . . may be all right!"

Fargo knew that wasn't what they were going to find. So did Harry, he suspected. But Harry couldn't allow himself to give up hope just yet, no matter how overwhelming the odds were.

In a quiet but steely voice, Fargo said, "Step back a little, Harry. I'll do this."

Harry sobbed but did as Fargo told him. Fargo tossed

several more rocks aside. There was no need for speed now. He could see part of Conway's chest. It wasn't rising and falling. Conway wasn't breathing.

Fargo grunted as he lifted a large piece of rock and threw it aside, revealing Conway's bloody and battered face. Conway was lying on his left side. His skull was misshapen from being crushed by the rocks. Behind Fargo, Harry made a noise of despair and turned away. A second later Fargo heard him retching.

Fargo touched Conway's shoulder and murmured, "I'm sorry, Frank. Sorry I couldn't get there in time."

There had been no time. The rockslide had been so sudden that no one could have prevented it. No one trapped in its path as Conway had been could have escaped. It was a tragic accident.

But Fargo's face was grim as he looked up at the top of the bluff and wondered if it really had been an accident.

His priorities had changed now. Before, he had needed to get to Frank Conway on the very slender chance that the man might still be alive. Now that he was sure Conway was dead, Fargo's attention turned to the avalanche itself. There had been no warning before the rocks started to fall, nothing to indicate that such a catastrophe was about to take place. When something happened so unexpectedly, especially in nature, you had to look closely at things to see if maybe the hand of man was involved.

Fargo stood up and turned away from Conway. He stepped over to Harry, who was on his knees at the edge of the stream. Fargo grasped Harry's arm and helped him to his feet.

"Come on, Harry," Fargo said. "You've got to be strong for Dinah now. She needs you."

"B-but Pa . . ."

Fargo urged Harry toward the wagon. Dinah was sitting on the ground now, slumped against one of the vehicle's wheels. She had her hands over her face and was shaking with the sobs that went through her.

"Your pa can stay right where he is for now," Fargo said. "You help Dinah. If you can, get her to lie down inside the wagon." He paused, then said, "I'm counting on you to protect her, Harry."

The grim note in Fargo's voice got through to Harry. He

looked at the Trailsman and said, "You . . . you think something else might happen?"

"I don't know. But I need to get up on top of that bluff and take a look around, see if I can tell what caused that avalanche."

"You think somebody started it on purpose?" Harry sounded horrified.

"I don't know," Fargo said again. "That's why I need you to look after Dinah."

"All right, Mr. Fargo. I . . . I can do it."

Fargo squeezed Harry's shoulder for a second. "I knew I could count on you."

Harry went to Dinah and knelt beside her while Fargo untied the Ovaro and swung up into the saddle. He sent the stallion galloping down the canyon. He remembered a place about a half-mile away where he could cross the stream and climb the slope on the other side that turned into the steep bluff above the Conway claim.

As he rode, he slid the Henry from its saddle sheath and levered a round into the rifle's chamber. If that rockslide had been deliberate, then whoever started it wanted to kill Frank Conway. The killer, or killers, could still be lurking around, and if that were the case, they wouldn't like it if Fargo started nosing around. He was going to be ready for trouble.

Less than half an hour later, he reached the top of the bluff. The ground up here was rocky dotted with scrubby pines and covered in places with sparse grass. One of the snowcapped peaks of the Sierra Nevadas loomed above it. So far since leaving the claim, Fargo hadn't seen anyone. He had run across a few hoofprints, but they were old, no telling when they'd been made. He noticed, however, that there was no game moving around in the woods, and the birds were silent. Those were good indications that somebody had passed through this way not long before.

If someone had been up here, they'd been good at covering their tracks. Fargo's keen eyes could spot a trail where few others could. He dismounted and let the Ovaro's reins dangle. On foot, he approached the edge of the bluff, making the approach slowly and carefully so he wouldn't disturb any sign that might have been left.

The stream had undercut the bluff a little to cause the

overhang. Above that the bluff sloped back to the top. The face of it was quite rugged, with dozens of protrusions of rock. Fargo hunkered on his haunches at the brink and studied the steep slope and the ground along the edge. For long minutes, nothing moved except his eyes.

The edge of the bluff was rocky, too, littered with stones ranging in size from pebbles to boulders. All anybody would have had to do was shove one of the good-sized rocks over the edge, and as it bounded down the slope it would take more and more of the others with it.

Fargo looked down at the wagon. He couldn't see Dinah anymore, but Harry was sitting on a log beside the campfire. Fargo hoped that meant Dinah was lying down inside the wagon, as he had suggested.

He straightened and moved along the bluff, his eyes once again studying the ground. When he reached the spot directly above the place where Frank Conway had died, he knelt once more. After a moment, he reached down toward the ground, but his fingers stopped short of the marks he saw there. To Skye Fargo, the faint indentations in the dirt told a damning story. Someone had crouched here, put his shoulder to the rock that had formed a small hollow in the ground during the scores, perhaps hundreds, of years it had sat there, and shoved hard enough to send it toppling over the brink. That was what had started the avalanche.

Frank Conway had been murdered. There was no doubt of that in Fargo's mind.

He was filled with a cold fury as he stood up. Murder always outraged him, no matter what the circumstances, but to have a friend like Frank Conway killed in cold blood right before his eyes . . . that was more than Fargo could swallow. Then and there, he vowed vengeance on whoever had been responsible for Conway's death.

Fargo stalked back to the Ovaro and mounted up. He checked the top of the bluff once more for tracks, but found none. The murderer had come up here on foot, Fargo decided. He couldn't have ridden a horse up here without leaving some sign that Fargo would have seen. Doubling back on his own trail, Fargo rode into the woods and began searching.

A short time later, he found fresh horse droppings in a grove of pines. The killer had left his mount here, then returned for it after starting the rock slide. Fargo spotted an impression of a boot heel on the ground. He swung down and looked at it more closely. The partial track was large enough and deep enough to indicate that a man had made it, but that was all Fargo could glean from it. The heel had no unusual markings.

He was able to backtrack from there. The killer had turned around and gone back the way he came. Fargo could tell that much from the hoofprints left by the horse. The trail led down to the stream. The killer's horse had splashed across the narrow brook, then turned east toward the creek it flowed into. Fargo followed the tracks that far, then bit back a curse of frustration as they merged with the hundreds of hoofprints and wagon tracks along the main trail that followed the creek up and down the valley. With all the prospectors coming and going over this path these days, there was no way to pick out the marks left by the killer.

Fargo wheeled the stallion and rode back toward the Conway claim. When he got there, he found Harry working to clear away more of the fallen rocks. The young man was dry-eyed now, but his face still carried the bleak stamp of grief.

"Dinah's in the wagon, like you said," Harry greeted Fargo. "It was a chore calming her down, but I did the best I could."

"I know you did, Harry," Fargo told him. "Let me give you a hand."

Working together, they finished uncovering Frank Conway's broken body. When that was done, they lifted the corpse and carried it across the creek to the grassy bank. After Conway had been laid out on the ground, Harry said, "I'll go get a blanket to wrap him in." His voice was hoarse and gruff with the effort of controlling his emotions. "Then I guess we'll have to dig a grave."

"Not just yet, Harry," Fargo said, making the words as gentle as possible. "We need to get Judge Boothe out here, and maybe Doc Parkhurst and Joe Patterson. There's a legal way of doing things in these parts now when there's a crime, and we need to follow it."

Harry frowned. "I don't understand. It was just an avalanche, wasn't it?"

Fargo shook his head and said, "I'm afraid not. I found

enough sign to tell me that somebody started it. Your father was murdered."

"Murdered," Harry repeated in hollow tones. "But who . . . who would do such a thing?"

"That's what I intend to find out," Fargo said.

Fargo didn't want to leave Dinah there by herself with her father's body, nor did he trust Harry to protect her if whoever killed Conway came back. That meant Harry had to ride to Ophir to fetch Judge Boothe and the others. He didn't want to go, but Fargo convinced him it was the only thing to do.

After Harry had trotted off on one of the draft horses, Fargo took a blanket from inside the wagon and used it to cover Conway's body. While looking over the tailgate into the wagon, he'd seen Dinah sleeping on a pallet on the floor of the vehicle. She was lying on her side, her knees pulled up, and her face was streaked with dried tears. Fargo thought she looked like a child in that position, and his heart went out to her. She had lost her mother, and now her father was gone, too. The fresh start the family had come to California for had turned bad after getting off to such a promising beginning.

Fargo took the pot of stew off the fire. No one had stirred it for a long time, and the smell of burned food filled the air. He set it aside to clean out later, then sat down on the log where Harry had been sitting earlier. Now there was nothing to do but wait.

A short time later, an abrupt cry came from inside the wagon. Fargo stood up and went over to the tailgate. He saw Dinah sitting up. A shudder went through her as she looked at him and said in a broken voice, "Oh, Skye, I had the most horrible dream . . . only it wasn't a dream, was it?"

"I'm afraid not," Fargo said.

Dinah began to cry again. "Wh-where's Harry?"

"He's gone to town to bring the judge and the doctor and the marshal out here."

"The doctor?" Dinah said, seizing on what must have seemed to her like a tiny sliver of hope.

Fargo shook his head. "I'm sorry, Dinah. Doc Parkhurst

is the closest thing Ophir has to a coroner, unless it's the undertaker. He may come along, too."

"I . . . I knew there was no chance, but I couldn't help thinking . . . just for a second . . ."

"I know," Fargo said. "I'm sorry."

Dinah took a deep breath and wiped away some of the tears. "Harry told me you were going to look up on the bluff and see if you could tell what happened. Did you find out anything?"

Fargo hesitated, then decided that there was no point in keeping the truth from her. "I found enough to tell me that someone started that rock slide deliberately."

"You mean . . . they killed Pa on purpose?"

Fargo nodded. "That's right. Your father was murdered."

Dinah looked straight at him, her gaze intent. "You're going to find out who did it, aren't you?"

"I'm going to do my best," Fargo promised.

"And when you do . . you'll kill them."

"That depends. I'll see that they're brought to justice, one way or the other."

Dinah nodded, accepting that answer. "I almost hope they don't come peacefully."

Fargo gave her a grim smile and said, "I know what you mean. I feel the same way."

She started to climb out of the wagon. "I have to tend to things. The stew—"

"I set it aside. I'm afraid it burned up."

"I'll clean the pot, then."

"That can wait," Fargo started to tell her. He stopped as he realized that she needed some chore to do, to keep her mind off what had happened. She had to grieve for the loss of her father, of course, but it wouldn't hurt for her to keep busy for a while.

The horse Harry had ridden into Ophir couldn't come close to matching the Ovaro's pace, and on the return trip Judge Boothe and Dr. Parkhurst would be traveling in a buggy. So Fargo wasn't surprised when it was past the middle of the afternoon by the time the delegation from Ophir arrived at the Conway claim. Harry was leading the way, with Joe Patterson riding alongside him and Boothe and Parkhurst bringing up the rear in the judge's buggy, as Fargo had expected.

Harry went to his sister as soon as he dismounted and hugged Dinah. "Are you all right?" he asked her.

She nodded. "As all right as I can be."

Joe Patterson was wearing a broad-brimmed black hat, and he had an old gun belt strapped around his waist. He swung down from the saddle and gave Fargo a curt nod. "Mighty bad business, from what the boy says."

"Yes, it is," Fargo agreed.

Parkhurst got down from the buggy and said in a quiet voice, "The, ah, deceased? . . ."

Fargo inclined his head toward the blanket-shroud form beside the creek.

While Parkhurst went to take a look at Conway's body, Judge Boothe joined Fargo and Patterson and ran his fingers through his tangled white beard. "I knew it was only a matter o' time until all hell broke loose again," he said, "but I figured it'd be in town, not out here."

"Why would somebody want to kill Conway?" Patterson asked. "I didn't really know him, but he seemed like a nice enough fella."

"I don't think that had anything to do with it," Fargo said. "His claim was showing good color. I think that's why he was killed."

Boothe frowned. "You figure somebody plans to jump this here claim?"

"No other reason I know of to drop a few tons of rock on top of him."

"There are still those two youngsters," Patterson pointed out. "I reckon the claim belongs to them now."

"I know. That's one of the things that's got me worried."

Fargo had already begun to wonder what Dinah and Harry would do now. They might be able to rebuild the sluice and work the claim themselves, but could they hold it against the human scavengers who might move in now that Conway was dead?

If that was what they wanted to do, Fargo decided, he would help them any way he could.

Parkhurst came back from examing the body. Pitching his voice so that Dinah and Harry couldn't overhear, he said, "I'd say the poor man died almost instantly. He was probably knocked unconscious by the first rock that hit him."

"That's small comfort, but better than nothin', I suppose," Patterson said. He looked at Fargo. "I ain't fool enough to think I can follow a trail that Skye Fargo can't. How do you suggest we find the critter or critters who did this?"

"The only thing we can do is keep our eyes and ears open," Fargo said. "Somebody knows what happened here. Sooner or later they'll make a slip, whoever they are."

Parkhurst said, "I'll hold an inquest, and I'm sure once they hear your testimony, Mr. Fargo, the jury will return a verdict of murder."

"And I'll issue a blank warrant for the skunks what done it," Judge Boothe put in.

"Can you do that?" Patterson asked.

"I can until somebody higher up tells me not to, and right now in this corner o' California, there ain't no higher authority except the Almighty His ownself."

A grim smile tugged at the corner of Fargo's mouth. What Boothe suggested was rather high-handed, but the judge had a point. The old mountain-man-turned-jurist was the law in these parts right now.

Boothe turned toward the wagon. "We better find out what Conway's kids want to do now."

The four men walked over to join Dinah and Harry. They all took their hats off, and the judge said, "I sure am sorry about what happened to your pa, you two. I know this is a mighty bad time to be pesterin' you with questions, but where do you reckon he'd have wanted to be laid to rest?"

Dinah looked around. "What about out here? This . . . this is the place we've spent the most time since we left Illinois. I know Pa liked it here." She summoned up a smile. "You couldn't ask for prettier surroundings."

"That's true enough, little lady," Boothe said. He looked at Parkhurst. "What do you think, Doc?"

Parkhurst shrugged. "I'd say it's up to them. No reason why the burial can't take place out here. It's nicer than that crowded little cemetery in town, that's for sure."

There were several shovels among the gear brought West by the Conways. Fargo and Patterson got a couple of them and went over to the edge of the trees to a spot Dinah pointed out. Harry agreed with her that it would make a suitable grave site. The ground was rather rocky and the digging was slow going, but by the time the sun was lowering toward the western horizon, Fargo and Patterson had been able to scoop out a hole long enough and deep enough.

Judge Boothe and Dr. Parkhurst took care of wrapping the body, using the blanket that had already been laid over the earthly remains of Frank Conway. Meanwhile, Harry hammered together a crude coffin, keeping his back turned to Boothe and Parkhurst as they went about their work. Dinah sat on the lowered tailgate of the wagon, watching Fargo and Patterson.

When everything was ready, the four men carried the coffin over to the grave and lowered it into the hole as gently as possible. They stepped back and removed their hats. After a moment of silence, Judge Boothe spoke. "The Good Book tells us man's fate is ashes to ashes and dust to dust. Not to dispute the Word o' the Lord, but I reckon there's more to it than that. A fella is more than the body he carries around with him. There's the heart and the soul that make him who he is, and the memories that he leaves behind in the hearts and souls of them what love him. This man here, Frank Conway, had two young'uns who loved him a whole heap. They still do, even though he's gone from this earth. I reckon that'll make him rest a sight easier, up yonder where he's gone for his eternal reward." The judge bowed his head. "So, Lord, we're askin' you to welcome Frank Conway, and I know he'd want You to look after these two fine children he's left behind. May God have mercy on us all. . . . Amen."

"Amen," Fargo echoed the benediction, along with Patterson and Parkhurst.

Dinah and Harry had stood with their arms around each other as Boothe spoke. Dinah rested her head against Harry's shoulder and sobbed. Fargo wished there was something he could do to ease her pain, but he knew time was the only thing that would heal the hurt of losing her father. Fargo had lost loved ones of his own in the past.

Boothe and Parkhurst urged Dinah and Harry back over to the wagon. Fargo and Patterson took up the shovels again and began filling in the grave. The hollow thud of dirt striking the coffin was an ugly sound, Fargo thought, one of the ugliest sounds in the world.

When it was done Patterson said, "I'll see that a marker's made and put up out here."

"I'm sure the kids will appreciate that."

Patterson looked toward Dinah and Harry as they stood beside the wagon and rubbed his jaw in thought. "You reckon those two ought to come back into town tonight? I ain't sure it'd be a good idea to leave them out here by themselves."

"They won't be by themselves," Fargo said. "I'll stay with them if they decide to stay. But I guess we ought to ask them what they want to do."

Patterson nodded in agreement. He and Fargo went over to the wagon and joined the others, only to find that Dinah and Harry had already been discussing their options with the judge and Dr. Parkhurst.

Boothe said, "Miss Dinah and young Harry here have decided to go back to Ophir for the night."

"I think that's a good idea," Fargo said.

Harry spoke up. "The man who . . . who started that avalanche—do you think he'll come back, Mr. Fargo?"

"He might." An idea occurred to Fargo. "As a matter of fact, I think I'll stay out here tonight, just in case he does."

Patterson frowned. "I ain't sure stayin' out here by yourself is a good idea. If there's more trouble—"

"If there's more trouble, someone needs to be here to handle it," Fargo said.

Patterson put his hand on the butt of his gun. "Yep. That's why I'm stayin', too."

Fargo saw that the liveryman/marshal wasn't going to be dissuaded. He grinned and said, "All right, Joe. I'll be glad to have the company."

Boothe said, "And me an' the doc will go with you youngsters into Ophir. Not to rush you, but we'd best get started. It'll be dark already, 'fore we can get back."

Fargo and Harry hitched the team to the wagon, then Harry and Dinah climbed into the seat and Harry took up the reins. They followed the buggy carrying Judge Boothe and Dr. Parkhurst. Both vehicles vanished down the canyon, leaving Fargo and Patterson at the campsite.

Patterson glanced toward the trees. The shadows were thick under the pines now, and the darkness reached out to touch the low mound of freshly turned earth that marked Frank Conway's final resting place.

"Does bein' this close to a grave make you a mite nervous, Fargo?"

The Trailsman shook his head. "I've been too close to death too many times for it to bother me. I have a healthy respect for the Grim Reaper, but I'm not afraid of him."

"Me, neither," Patterson said, but he didn't sound a hundred percent convinced.

As night fell, the two men built up the fire and shared a supper of jerky from Fargo's saddlebags and some biscuits that Dinah had left behind for them. The Ovaro and Patterson's horse, both hobbled, grazed on the grass along the bank of the stream. After eating, Patterson filled his pipe and puffed clouds of smoke into the air. "How was this claim workin' out for Conway?" he asked Fargo.

"He said he was finding good color, and Harry and Dinah told me the same thing. I don't know exactly how much gold they'd taken out of the creek, but they seemed to think it was enough to make the claim worthwhile."

"So it'd be worth jumpin'?"

"More than likely," Fargo agreed.

Patterson chewed on the stem of his briar. "I'm the marshal of Ophir, so I don't know that I've got any real jurisdiction out here. But I don't intend to see the polecat who murdered Conway get away with it."

"Neither do I."

"We'd better keep a watch tonight."

"All right. I'll take the first one."

Patterson settled down in the bedroll he'd borrowed from Harry Conway, and within a few minutes his snores were filling the air. Fargo sat by the fire, careful not to stare into the lowering flames, and listened to the night. All the small sounds that came to his ears were normal enough. Peace reigned over this corner of the Sierra Nevadas.

Fargo thought about Natalie Talmadge. She might miss him when he didn't show up at the Top-Notch tonight. A part of him hoped she would. But she would have heard about the avalanche that had taken Conway's life, and she could guess that this was where he was, watching over the claim for Dinah and Harry. Fargo didn't know if Natalie was the jealous type or not. He was pretty sure she didn't have any idea what had happened between him and Dinah in the loft of the livery stable. If she did know, would she care? Fargo couldn't answer that.

The minutes stretched into hours. Fargo had no trouble staying awake. A life lived on the edge of danger had taught him how to remain alert for however long was necessary, no matter how tired he became. Even when the time came for him to sleep, he knew that a part of his senses would remain keenly attuned to anything that might warn of trouble. That was the way it always was, and although from time to time he might wish things were different, he knew they never would be as long as he continued the sort of life he led.

Far into the night, he put a hand on Patterson's shoulder and shook him awake. Patterson sat up, stretched, yawned, and asked, "Anything goin' on?"

"It's been quiet," Fargo told him. "Looks like whoever rolled those rocks down on Conway isn't coming back tonight."

"Maybe they figured it was too soon to make another move."

"Maybe," Fargo said, "but they'll be back. After committing murder for a chance to get their hands on this claim, they're not going to just abandon their plans."

"And when they move in, we've got 'em."

"That's right," Fargo said.

But as he rolled up in his blankets to get a few hours of sleep, he thought that it probably wouldn't work out in such a neat and simple fashion.

Somehow, it never did.

8

The last part of the night passed as quietly as the first part had, and after eating breakfast the next morning, Fargo and Patterson saddled up and started back to Ophir.

When they arrived, they found the Conway wagon parked behind Patterson's livery stable. "Dickie must've told 'em it was all right to leave it there," Patterson said, referring to the young man who worked for him. "The kids are down at the hotel, maybe, or one of the boardin' houses."

"I'll find them," Fargo said. He lifted a hand in farewell as Patterson dismounted and led his horse into the livery barn.

As Fargo rode down the street, he saw Omar Sprague tacking a piece of paper to one of the posts that supported the awning over the boardwalk. Turning the Ovaro closer to the building, Fargo read the words printed on the paper: VOTE FOR PROGRESS. VOTE FOR SPRAGUE. Fargo grinned. It appeared that the campaign for mayor was about to heat up a mite.

"Morning, Sprague," Fargo called to the storekeeper.

Sprague lowered his hammer and turned around. "Oh, hello, Fargo," he said. "Say, that was a terrible thing about Frank Conway. I heard that you were there when it happened."

Fargo rested his hands on his saddle horn and leaned forward. He nodded and said, "Yes, I was there. I saw Conway murdered. There was nothing I could do to stop it."

Sprague shook his head. "Horrible, just horrible." He gestured with the hammer in his hand. "It just goes to show you that we've got to establish law and order around here. Thank God for Judge Boothe."

"If we can find out who was responsible for Conway's death, he'll be brought to justice. There's no doubt of that."

"We?" Sprague repeated. "You're still working with Marshall Patterson?"

"That's right."

"Well, I wish you luck."

Fargo nodded toward the handbill Sprague had just put up. "Looks like you've decided you want the job of mayor after all."

"Someone has to do it," Sprague said. "I don't think Doc really wants the job."

"Probably not. He feels like he has his hands full already."

"Don't we all?"

Fargo didn't say anything to that. He turned the Ovaro and nudged the stallion on down the street. He rode to Dr. Parkhurst's office, dismounted, and went inside. He found the doctor sitting across a checkerboard from Judge Boothe.

The judge glanced at Fargo, then jumped three of Parkhurst's checkers and cackled with laughter. "Mornin', Fargo," he said. "You must've brung me some good luck. I ain't beat this sawbones yet."

"And you're not going to now," Parkhurst said. He reached for the board and jumped five of Boothe's checkers. "That's it. I win again."

Boothe stared at the board for a second, then said, "Goldurn it, I thought I had you that time!"

Fargo reversed one of the chairs and straddled it. "Where did Dinah and Harry spend the night?" he asked.

Boothe and Parkhurst looked more solemn as they were reminded of Frank Conway's death. Boothe said, "They're down at Miz Lemmon's boardin' house. I planned on runnin' that Roosky outta the room we been sharin' at the hotel and givin' it to Miss Dinah, but Miz Lemmon said she'd find a place for 'em. From what I hear, the cookin' won't be as good, but it'll do."

Parkhurst asked, "Did anything else happen last night out at their claim?"

Fargo shook his head. "Nope. Quiet as could be. Joe said he figured whoever killed Conway thought it was too soon to try anything else, and he's probably right."

Boothe took out his pipe and started filling it. "I had me a talk with them young'uns last night, and I ain't sure they're goin' back out there. Too many bad memories. Besides, it'd be askin' a lot of a couple of kids to run a minin' claim by themselves."

Fargo frowned. "You mean they're going to give it up?"

"That's how it sounded to me."

Fargo hated to hear that. It meant that whoever had killed Frank Conway had accomplished what he'd set out to do, which was to get the family off the claim. Fargo felt certain of that. Still, he couldn't really blame Dinah and Harry for feeling that way. If it was just a matter of the work involved in rebuilding the sluice and getting the mining operation going again, Fargo could help them with that. Sooner or later, though, he would have to ride on, and then the two young people would be left on their own. Maybe it would be better if they tried something else. They could even go back to Illinois if they decided they wanted to do that. Fargo had felt from the first that coming to California had been mostly Frank Conway's idea.

"I'll talk with them, but when you come right down to it, they have to do whatever they think is best."

Boothe nodded. "Yep, that's what I figure, too, and Doc here agrees with me."

Fargo stood up. "Where's this boarding house? I'll go see them right now."

Parkhurst told him how to find Mrs. Lemmon's place and Fargo set off toward it on foot, leaving the Ovaro tied at the hitch rack in front of the doctor's office. He went up the other side of the street from Sprague's store, but as he passed the emporium, he spotted the familiar shine of honey-blonde hair and looked over to see Dinah going into the store. Fargo paused, frowning a little, then started across the street himself, stepping around the muddy patches left from the last rain several days earlier.

As he came into the emporium, he paused for a second to let his eyes adjust to the dimness inside the big, cavernous building. When he could see better, he walked toward the counter in the rear of the store. Dinah stood there, talking to Omar Sprague.

"—sure you won't be disappointed," she was saying. "I worked for years in my father's store back home."

Sprague rubbed his short beard and frowned in thought. "Well, I don't know—"

Dinah turned as she heard Fargo's footsteps. "Skye!" she said, a smile coming to her face. After the tragedy of the day before, Fargo was glad to see that she could still smile.

He nodded to her. "Hello, Dinah. What are you doing?"

She looked more serious. "I was just asking Mr. Sprague for a job here at his emporium."

"I don't have any female clerks," Sprague said. "I'm not sure I ever heard of such a thing."

Dinah turned back to him. "Women work in stores all the time back East," she said. "I hope you'll give me a chance, Mr. Sprague."

Fargo said, "You've decided not to go back out to the claim, then?"

"Harry and I had a long talk about it last night," Dinah told him. "We decided we can't handle it alone. We're both going to try to get work here in town."

What she was saying made sense, Fargo thought, yet in a way he still couldn't help but be disappointed. Dinah and Harry would never get rich working at menial jobs in Ophir. On the other hand, it would be less dangerous for them here in town. And they had a right to make up their minds for themselves, Fargo reminded himself. On yet another hand, he hadn't told them that he was willing to help them work the claim.

He did so now, saying, "Dinah, if you and Harry want to go back out there, I'll go with you. I'll stay and help you with the claim as long as you want me around."

"Oh, Skye." She laid a hand on his arm. "That's sweet of you, but I . . . I just don't think I can stand it." A small shudder went through her. "Every time I looked at that bluff looming over the place, I'd hear that awful rumble in my head and see all those rocks falling down—"

Her voice caught and tears glistened in her eyes. Fargo said, "That's all right, Dinah. You don't have to explain. I understand."

"Thank you." She turned back to the storekeeper. "Well, Mr. Sprague, what about it? I promise you I'm a good worker."

"I suppose I could give you a chance," Sprague said in grudging tones. "Lord knows I could use some dependable help. Hardly a week goes by that one of my clerks doesn't decide to up and quit and go back to prospecting."

"Thank you. I won't let you down."

"I don't have any work for that brother of yours, though," Sprague said. "The store's not that busy. He'll have to find something somewhere else."

"He's out looking around town now. He said he'd just as soon not work in a store again, since he did that back home."

Fargo asked, "What's Harry going to do?"

Dinah shook her head. "I don't know. But I'm sure he'll find something."

Fargo frowned as he remembered Walt Drummond telling Harry to come see him when he grew up. After losing his father, Harry might feel that he was grown up now, and working around a saloon would have a powerful appeal to a youngster who was fascinated by such things, as most young men were. Of course, Drummond would probably just run him off if Harry came looking for a job, but there might still be trouble. It had been only a couple of days since Harry's run-in with the gambler Tom Harlin.

"Skye?" Dinah said, seeing his expression. "What's wrong?"

"Just thinking about something," Fargo said. "And I'd better go tend to it while it's on my mind." He took her hand for a second and squeezed it. "I'll see you later."

"You know we're staying down at Mrs. Lemmon's boarding house?"

Fargo nodded. "Doc and the judge told me."

Sprague rubbed his hands together and said, "Well, Miss Conway, if you're ready to get to work, I've got some bolts of cloth in the back that just came in and need sorting."

Fargo smiled at Dinah, touched a finger to the brim of his hat, and turned to walk out of the emporium. When he reached the street, he looked up and down for any sign of Harry Conway. Not seeing any, he started toward Drummond's Gold Bar.

To get there, he had to pass the Top-Notch, and as he was doing so, the door of that saloon opened and Natalie Talmadge stepped out onto the boardwalk, dressed in a dark-blue gown and hat. She stopped and said in a cool voice, "Hello, Skye."

Fargo took off his hat. "Natalie." He couldn't tell if she was angry or not.

"I thought you'd stop by last night. When you didn't, I got a little worried."

"Sorry to hear that," Fargo said. He didn't feel like explaining himself, didn't feel that he owed Natalie any explanations.

Her expression softened a little. "I heard about what happened out at the claim of those people you met on the way here. It must have been terrible, seeing that poor man killed that way."

"I've seen a lot of people die," Fargo said. "But I reckon you never really get used to it. At least, I hope I never do."

"You won't." The look in Natalie's eyes grew even more compassionate. "You're a good man, Skye Fargo. Some people think you're hard and dangerous, and I've seen enough with my own eyes to know that you can be both of those things. But the biggest thing about you is your heart." Her eyes dropped for a second to his groin. "Although it's not the biggest by much, mind you."

Fargo had to chuckle. "I'll come by tonight if I can," he promised.

"You do that. I'll have a special supper waiting for you."

"I won't forget."

Natalie walked on down the boardwalk. Fargo watched her with appreciation. She was a beautiful woman, one of the loveliest he had ever met.

Then he strode toward Drummond's Gold Bar, still intent on the errand that had brought him in this direction to start with.

Because of the big windows, it was lighter in the saloon at this time of day than it was in Sprague's emporium. Fargo didn't have to pause to let his eyes adjust as he pushed through the batwings. Right away, he spotted Harry Conway standing at the bar, talking to Walt Drummond. The Gold Bar wasn't very busy this early in the day. Three men leaned on the bar, nursing drinks poured for them by a solitary bartender. At one of the tables, Tom Harlin sat dealing a hand of solitaire. Those five men were the only ones in the place other than Drummond and Harry. Fargo figured all the girls were upstairs asleep.

Harry was facing away from Fargo and talking to Drummond. He didn't look around until Drummond glanced over his shoulder at Fargo. Then Harry looked back and started a little, surprised to see Fargo there. His expression was more than a little guilty, too, as if he'd been caught at something he didn't want anybody to know about.

"Hello, Harry," Fargo said, his voice soft in the hushed atmosphere of the saloon. From the other side of the room, the cards whispered as Tom Harlin dealt them onto the green felt.

"Mr. Fargo," Harry said. "I didn't expect to run into you here."

"No, I don't suppose you did."

Drummond said, "Something I can do for you, Fargo? You want a drink? If you don't, you'd better move along, because I'm talking business here."

"What business do you have with a sixteen-year-old boy, Drummond?"

"I'm seventeen!" Harry said. "Well . . . almost."

"This fine young man stopped by here to ask me for a job," Drummond said. "I don't see that that's any concern of yours, Fargo."

"Harry's my friend. I think he'd be better off not working for the likes of you."

Drummond had been leaning one elbow on the bar. At Fargo's words, he straightened, and his features stiffened into an angry mask.

"Like I said, if you don't want a drink, you'd better move along, Fargo."

Fargo jerked a thumb toward the table where the gambler sat. "How does Harlin feel about you hiring Harry? A couple of days ago he was ready to plug him over a spilled drink."

Drummond raised an eyebrow. "You know, that's an interesting question. Let's ask him." He turned his head toward Harlin. "Tom, do you mind if I hire this kid?"

Without looking up from his solitaire spread, Harlin said, "Whatever you want to do is all right with me, Walt. You know that."

"That's what I thought." Drummond looked at Fargo again. "There's your answer. Tom doesn't mind, the kid wants to work here, and I think it's a good idea. So you lose all around."

Fargo looked at the young man. "Harry—"

114

"I have to do something to earn money, Mr. Fargo. Dinah and I can't work that gold claim. We . . . we don't even want to go back out there. Not after what happened to Pa. Can't you see that?"

Fargo understood, all right. He didn't agree with the way Harry had decided to handle the situation but Fargo knew it wasn't his decision to make. He took a deep breath and then nodded. "All right, Harry. I just hope you know what you're getting into." He asked Drummond, "What exactly do you intend to have Harry doing? Swamping out the place?"

"No, I've got an old drunk for that. There's plenty to do around here. I've always got errands that need running, and the kid can fill in behind the bar when we're shorthanded." Drummond clapped a hand on Harry's shoulder. "Don't worry, kid. I'll keep you busy."

"Thanks, Mr. Drummond."

Fargo wondered just how much of Drummond's decision to hire Harry was based on the fact that the saloonkeeper knew Fargo didn't like the idea. There had been friction between Fargo and Drummond from the moment they'd met. The two men seemed to feel an instinctive dislike for each other.

With a shake of his head, Fargo turned to walk out of the Gold Bar. Harry said, "Mr. Fargo, wait a minute!", and hurried after him. Over his shoulder, Harry threw the words, "I'll be right back, Mr. Drummond."

Harry caught up to Fargo on the boardwalk outside the saloon. He reached out and caught hold of Fargo's sleeve. Fargo didn't like being grabbed, but he suppressed the irritation he felt.

"What is it, Harry?"

"You don't understand, Mr. Fargo," Harry said, pitching his voice so low that he couldn't be overhead inside the saloon. "I've been thinking about what . . . about what happened to Pa. That's why I came to ask Mr. Drummond for a job."

Fargo frowned. "I don't see what you're getting at."

"That man Gratton and his gang, you said you thought he might work for Mr. Drummond. And the more I thought about it, the more it seemed like killing Pa was something Gratton might do."

Understanding dawned inside Fargo. He considered Gratton a likely suspect in Frank Conway's murder, too, and he had wondered about a possible connection with Drummond.

"You're trying to find out if Drummond had anything to do with your father's death," he said to Harry.

The youngster nodded. "That's right. I figure if he did, I can poke around and find out about it."

"That's a good way to get yourself killed."

"But I have to do it. I have to find out the truth. That's why I have to get Mr. Drummond to trust me. That's why I have to do this—please don't hurt me, Mr. Fargo—"

With that, Harry cocked a fist and swung it at Fargo's head.

Fargo wasn't taken by surprise often, but he was now. Still, his instincts reacted in plenty of time for him to dodge the blow. Harry swung again. By now, Fargo had figured out what he was up to. Fargo ducked under the wild, looping punch and sent a short, straight right into Harry's belly. He pulled the punch as much as he could and still make it look real. The blow landed with enough force to knock the wind out of Harry and make him double over, his face turning pale. Fargo caught hold of his coat collar, jerked him upright, and marched him back into the Gold Bar, where Drummond, Harlin, and the others in the saloon had been able to see the exchange of blows through the big plate-glass windows.

Fargo gave Harry a shove that sent him stumbling toward Drummond. He said, "Since this crazy pup works for you now, Drummond, I'll hold you responsible for keeping him away from me."

Drummond caught hold of Harry's arm and steadied him. Harlin looked on with intense interest. "Get out of here, Fargo," Drummond said. "You're not welcome in the Gold Bar any longer."

"Leaving is my pleasure. I don't care for the smell in here."

Fargo turned and stalked out of the saloon, pushing the batwings aside with a little more force than was necessary. Knowing that Drummond and the others couldn't see him, he grinned.

There, he thought, that ought to convince Drummond

that any friendship between him and Harry Conway was finished.

For the next few days, life in Ophir was eventful but not overly violent. Judge Boothe held his first session of court, conducting it in an open-air, makeshift courtroom underneath a large tree at the edge of town. Charges ranging from disturbing the peace to petty theft to assault were brought against a dozen defendants, none of whom asked for a jury trial or put up much of a defense. The judge quickly and rightfully found all of them guilty. He levied fines for the minor convictions and sentenced one man to a month in jail for breaking a plank over another man's head without any warning. Joe Patterson's planned jail was still in the early stages of construction, so the convicted man would have to be locked up in his tack room. Under the circumstances, Judge Boothe ruled that it wouldn't be out of line for Patterson to put the man to work, since he had to be there at the stable anyway.

"Might as well get a little free labor out of the son of a gun," Boothe said before he adjourned the court. "Find the filthiest stalls you got and have him muck 'em out."

"I'll do that, Your Honor," Patterson agreed.

Quite a crowd turned out for the proceedings. Having an honest-to-goodness court in Ophir was a novelty, and folks enjoyed anything that broke up the monotony of day-to-day life on the frontier. The only thing better would have been a hanging, and most people agreed the judge would get around to that sooner or later.

Fargo stood at the rear of the crowd and watched. In his job as unofficial deputy—a post that seemed to have fallen to him whether he wanted it or not—he had helped Patterson corral some of the hell-raisers who were being tried today. When Boothe had banged his gravel down on the table set up under the tree and declared that court was adjourned, Fargo made his way forward while most of the bystanders drifted away.

Boothe grinned up at him. "What did you think, Fargo?" the judge asked.

"You ran things just fine, Judge," Fargo said. "You were firm but fair. Word will get around that folks have to behave themselves in Ophir now."

Boothe stroked his white beard. "I hope so. This place is well on its way to bein' a civilized law-abidin' town. Soon as we get a mayor elected next week, that'll be the last step."

Fargo wasn't certain an election would finish off the job of civilizing the boomtown, but he didn't argue with the judge.

"Why don't you come by Sprague's store this evenin'?" Boothe went on. "The town council's holdin' another meetin'."

"Last time I checked, I wasn't a member," Fargo said with a wry grin.

Boothe waved a knobby-knuckled hand. "That don't matter. Joe Patterson's a good man, but everybody knows it's really you who's put the fear o' God into the lawbreakers around here."

Fargo tried not to frown. He didn't want the responsibility of being a town-tamer. That was why he had turned down the job of marshal. It was bad enough that he was helping Patterson maintain order. When the time came for him to ride on, he wanted to be able to do it with a clear conscience.

But that day wasn't going to come any time soon, he sensed. Too many mysteries still bound him to Ophir. There was the attempt to burn down Natalie Talmadge's saloon, for one thing. Though the men who had lit the fire were dead, whoever had put them up to it was still on the loose. And Fargo couldn't forget the murder of Frank Conway. Whoever was responsible for that had to be brought to justice.

He still felt there was a connection between both those crimes and the hardcase called Gratton. Walt Drummond was still a suspect as far as Fargo was concerned, too, at least in the case of the fire. No, he told himself, he wasn't going to be leaving Ophir, so he might as well keep an eye on the town council's activities.

"I'll be there," he told Judge Boothe.

"Good. Come by 'round seven o'clock."

That was all right with Fargo. He could attend the meeting and still get to the Top-Notch in time for a late supper with Natalie—among other things.

When he arrived at the emporium a little before seven,

118

he found Joe Patterson waiting at the door. Patterson told Fargo, "Go on in, Skye. Nearly the whole bunch is already here."

"What about you?" Fargo asked.

"Oh. I'm supposed to stay out here so I can tell folks the store's closed and keep everybody out except the council members. And you, of course."

This time, Fargo did frown. Something about this setup rubbed him the wrong way. The only way to find out what was off-kilter about it, though, was to go inside and see what the town council was doing.

He heard angry voices as he stepped into the building. The dozen or so men who made up Ophir's town council were gathered at the back of the store. Judge Boothe was sitting on the counter, and he tried to make peace by saying, "Here now! Stop all that yellin', you jaspers! This ain't no way to conduct the town's business!"

The men ignored him. The council seemed to be divided into two opposing groups. The smaller one consisted of Omar Sprague and three other men. Sprague was jawing with Doc Parkhurst. Both of them were perspiring, redfaced, and angry.

Judge Boothe spotted Fargo striding along the aisle toward the rear of the store and raised his bushy white eyebrows in a silent plea for the Trailsman to do something. Fargo came up behind the squabbling council members and said, "Hold it!"

His deep, powerful voice rang out and brought quiet where the judge's had failed. The councilmen looked around at him in surprise.

"What's going on here?" Fargo demanded into the sudden silence.

"Law and order, that's what," Sprague snapped.

Doc Parkhurst snorted in disgust. "Out-and-out vigilantism is what you mean."

Sprague swung around toward and said, "Then what do you suggest, Doctor?" Scorn dripped from the merchant's words.

"Both of you be quiet," Fargo said. He looked at Boothe. "Judge, maybe you'd better explain things."

"I'll be glad to try," Booth said. He gestured at Sprague. "Mr. Sprague here has suggested that we move to close

119

down some o' Ophir's business. Some o' the fellas agree with him and the rest don't."

"What sort of businesses?" Fargo asked.

"The saloons, for one," Sprague said. "And the gambling dens and houses of ill repute, too."

A smile tugged at the corners of Fargo's mouth. "You do away with those places and you won't have much of a town left."

Sprague didn't see the humor in it. He said, "Perhaps not, but what is left will be law-abiding."

"There's no law against drinking and gambling." Fargo looked at Boothe. "Is there, Judge?"

Boothe pursed his lips. "'Well, not now, there ain't. But the council could vote to enact ord'nances that would ban all sorts o' things."

"And that's exactly what I've suggested that we do," Sprague said. "Once those laws are put into effect, we can run troublemakers like Walt Drummond and hussies like Natalie Talmadge out of our town."

Fargo's spine stiffened with anger. "Ophir is their town, too."

Sprague glared at him. "I'm surprised you'd defend Drummond, as much trouble as you've had with him yourself. But you've patronized Mrs. Talmadge's establishment quite a bit, I'm told, so it comes as no shock that you're speaking up on her behalf."

Fargo reined in his temper. Sprague was pompous and annoying, but he wasn't worth getting mad at, he told himself.

Parkhurst spoke up. "Any town needs laws, but I think it's a mistake to put them in just to run off certain businesses. That's the behavior of vigilantes."

One of the men who supported Sprague's suggestion said, "Maybe what we need are some vigilantes. Maybe we ought to just burn out Drummond and the Talmadge woman, rather than forcing them out with laws."

Boothe pointed a finger at the man and said, "That'll be enough o' *that,* mister! I'm gonna forget I just heard you proposin' arson and mayhem, but you damned well better not let me hear it again!"

Sprague held up both hands. "All right, all right, maybe we all need to cool off a little. All I did was make a suggestion. If the council doesn't agree with it, they can vote it down."

"I don't agree," Parkhurst said. "And if we're putting it to a vote, I vote 'no.' "

"So do I," one of the men with him said, and then another and another chimed in, agreeing. A moment later, when all the men had spoken up, it was obvious that Sprague's proposal had been defeated by a vote of six to four.

Sprague shrugged. "There you are, all legal and aboveboard." He looked at Parkhurst and went on in an icy voice, "You don't have to worry, Doctor. There won't be any vigilantes in Ophir . . . yet."

"What does that mean?" Parkhurst snapped.

"It means that we're willing to let you do things your way for now, but if it doesn't work . . . if the lawlessness in town gets worse instead of better . . . I'm sure the good men of Ophir will rise up and do whatever is necessary to restore order. And once I'm the mayor, I think it's only natural that support for my policies will grow stronger among the citizens."

Parkhurst narrowed his eyes. "Maybe you won't *be* mayor."

"We'll let the people decide," Sprague said with confidence.

Fargo hated this sort of political infighting, but he was relieved that Sprague's proposal had been voted down. It was true that a lot of the crime in a town usually centered on its saloons and gambling dens and brothels. But Fargo didn't believe in tarring all such establishments with the same brush. The Top-Notch was well run and peaceful most of the time. Even if he hadn't been taken with Natalie, he would have felt the same opposition to running the place out of business. For that matter, Drummond kept things under control in the Gold Bar, too.

Still, Fargo remembered the way Tom Harlin had shot down that prospector in broad daylight on the town's main street. Without saloons, Harlin wouldn't have been in Ophir, and that man might still be alive. Deciding where to draw the line—or whether there should be a line in the first place—was a thorny problem.

Sooner or later, he thought, Sprague would cause trouble

for Natalie and the other saloonkeepers. The man was so sure of himself that he would find a way. Fargo thought it might be a good idea to warn her of what was coming, but he also knew Natalie was intelligent enough that she probably had a good idea already. Any time a town started getting civilized, it didn't bode well for the saloons.

The council meeting broke up shortly after that without any clear-cut resolutions. Fargo lingered on the boardwalk with Judge Boothe and Dr. Parkhurst. Joe Patterson joined them.

"I heard some o' that," Patterson said. "Sounds like Omar wants to really clean up the town."

"How do you feel about that, Joe?" Parkhurst asked.

Patterson shook his head. "I agreed to be the marshal, which means I'll do my best to enforce whatever you boys say are the laws. But I'd just as soon leave folks alone if they ain't botherin' nothin'."

"That's exactly the way I feel," Parkhurst said. "I can see I'm going to have to win that election."

"Well, you got my vote, Doc," Patterson said with a grin.

Fargo said good night to the three men and started toward the Top-Notch. As he walked across the street and up the block, he thought about Dinah Conway. He had talked to her only briefly since she'd taken the job at the emporium, and although she claimed to be doing fine, he wasn't convinced. He had halfway hoped she would be at Sprague's tonight, but he didn't really expect her to be there. Sure enough, she hadn't been. Maybe he would go down to Mrs. Lemmon's boarding house before he went to the Top-Notch, he thought. Just to say hello. He wanted to talk to Harry, too, and see if the youngster had found out anything to connect Drummond with his father's murder.

Before Fargo could reach the boarding house, he heard the drumming of hoofbeats in the gathering dusk. Looking up the street, he saw a rider galloping into town and realized with a shock that it was Harry Conway. Fargo stopped and lifted a hand, catching Harry's eye. The young man hauled his mount to a sliding stop. Harry's eyes were wide and he was breathing hard. Something had happened, and Fargo was willing to bet it wasn't anything good.

"Hold on there, Harry," Fargo said. "What's wrong?"

"Out . . . out at the claim," Harry said, breathless from

the hard ride. "There are men there. One of 'em took a shot at me!"

"Did you see who it was?" Fargo asked, putting aside for the moment his surprise that Harry had returned to the gold claim.

"Yeah. Yeah, I did." Harry wiped the back of his hand across his mouth. "It was that bastard Gratton."

9

"Gratton," Fargo repeated, his voice cold and angry. All along, he had suspected that Gratton had something to do with the avalanche that killed Frank Conway. The fact that Gratton had now moved in on the claim wasn't exactly proof of anything but it was one more strong indication that Fargo was right.

Harry was still trying to catch his breath. Fargo motioned for him to get down from the horse. Harry did so, stepping up onto the boardwalk next to Fargo.

"What were you doing out there?" Fargo asked.

"Dinah picked some flowers somewhere and asked me to ride out there and put 'em on Pa's grave," Harry explained. "Mr. Drummond said it was all right, that he didn't need me this afternoon, so I did what Dinah asked. Only when I got there, I found Gratton and some of his men working the sluice. They'd cleared off the rocks and rebuilt it. When he saw me coming, Gratton yelled at me that I was trespassing, grabbed a rifle, and shot at me."

"How close did his shot come to you?"

"It went over my head—but close enough that I could hear it."

Fargo's jaw tightened. From what Harry said, he was pretty sure Gratton had been trying to scare the youngster, rather than kill him, but if Gratton's aim had been off even a little, Harry could have easily wound up dead.

Recalling that he and Harry had staged a falling out for Drummond's benefit, Fargo said, "You'd better get back over to the Gold Bar. I'll ride out to the claim tomorrow and have a talk with Gratton."

"More than likely he'll shoot at you, too, Mr. Fargo."

"I almost hope he does," Fargo said. He started to turn

away, then stopped as a thought occurred to him. "What happened to the flowers?"

Harry looked down at the boardwalk in shame. "I'm afraid I dropped 'em when I got my horse turned around and lit a shuck out of there."

"That's all right. There'll be other chances to put flowers on your pa's grave."

"Dinah's going to be mad at me when she hears about this."

"I don't think so. It wasn't your fault."

"Would you talk to her, Mr. Fargo?"

"I was planning to anyway. I'll tell her what happened."

"I'm much obliged to you." Harry stepped off the boardwalk and caught up the reins of his horse. He started leading it down the street toward the Gold Bar, postponing taking the mount back to the corral behind Mrs. Lemmon's boarding house until Fargo had had a chance to talk to Dinah.

Fargo cast a glance at the Top-Notch as he strode past the saloon. Natalie was waiting for him in there, but he had promised Harry he'd tell Dinah what had happened out at the claim. So far, Natalie seemed to be pretty understanding whenever he didn't show up when he was supposed to. Fargo hoped she stayed that way and didn't run out of patience with him. Either way, though, he was going to do what he thought was right.

A few minutes later, he was knocking on the door of the boarding house. Mrs. Lemmon, a plump widow with graying blond hair, answered the summons and smiled at the Trailsman. "Good evening, Mr. Fargo," she said. "Have you come to see Dinah?"

Fargo took off his hat. "That's right, ma'am. Is she in?"

Mrs. Lemmon stepped back to let Fargo into the house. "She's in the parlor. You go right in and make yourself at home."

Fargo hung his hat on a rack in the foyer and stepped into the parlor, where he found Dinah sitting on a divan and mending a shirt by lamplight. Fargo recognized the shirt as one of Harry's.

"Hello, Skye," Dinah said, her face lighting up with a smile. "What brings you here tonight? I'm not complaining, of course. We've hardly gotten to see each other lately."

"No, and that's a shame," Fargo said as he sat down beside her. "I'm not here just for a visit, though. I've got some news."

Worry sprang up in Dinah's eyes. "Is it about Harry? He should be back any time. He went out to . . . to the claim . . ."

"He's back. I saw him just a few minutes ago. But he wasn't able to put those flowers on your father's gave like you'd planned. Gratton and some of those other hardcases were out there. Gratton took a shot at Harry and ran him off."

Dinah's hand went to her mouth in surprise and alarm. "Harry!" she exclaimed. "Is he all right?"

Fargo nodded. "He wasn't hurt at all, just spooked. But he said Gratton and his bunch have taken over the claim, rebuilt the sluice, and are working it."

Anger flared in Dinah's eyes, joining the worry that was already there. "Those . . . those bastards! How dare they!"

"You and Harry *did* give up the claim," Fargo pointed out. "By not going back out there, you left it open for somebody else to come in and start working it."

"That was just what Gratton wanted when he killed Pa."

Fargo nodded. "I suspect you're right, but we don't know that for sure. Doesn't matter, though. I'm still going to ride out there tomorrow and have a talk with Gratton about taking a shot at Harry."

"But, Skye, if you go out there alone, Gratton will try to kill you. He hates you and has ever since that first day when you gave him that beating."

"I'm not going alone," Fargo assured her. "I thought I'd take Joe Patterson with me, maybe a few of the other men from town. It'll be an official delegation that calls on Gratton."

"Will that go any good?"

Fargo could only shake his head. "I don't know. But we can't let this pass without at least trying to get to the bottom of it."

"No, of course not. I realize now that maybe Harry and I should have stayed out there . . ."

"It was your decision," Fargo said. "And no one can say that you did the wrong thing."

"Maybe not. But this way, Gratton didn't really jump the claim. Can the law do anything to him?"

"Legally, he may not be a claim jumper. But there's still a law against murder, and Judge Boothe will see that it's enforced."

Dinah leaned against him, resting her head on his shoulder. "I wish you could stay with me tonight," she whispered. "It would mean so much to have you hold me and make love to me." She lifted her face to his. "Maybe I could come over to the livery stable later . . ."

Fargo thought about Natalie Talmadge and shook his head. "I don't think that would be a very good idea. If you and Harry plan to make Ophir your home, you don't need to get mixed up with somebody like me who'll have to move on."

"You wouldn't have to."

Fargo thought about the wild, untamed places and how they called out to him. "Yes, I would," he said softly. "Sooner or later, I would."

Dinah lowered her head to his shoulder again, and he tightened his arm around her. They had this moment, Fargo thought, and then that was probably the end of it.

Fargo had lived with endings all his life. They were never easy.

But there were always new trails to ease the way.

He climbed the rear stairs of the Top-Notch and went to Natalie's room. When he knocked on her door, she called, "Come in."

Fargo stopped just inside the room and eased the door closed behind him. He grinned when he saw her. "How did you know it was me?"

Natalie was stretched out on the bed, nude and lovely. She smiled at Fargo and said, "I thought you had stayed away from me about as long as you could possibly stand it, Skye."

"You're right about that," Fargo murmured as he moved toward the bed. The room was lit only by a lamp with its flame turned low. He dropped his hat on the dressing table and pulled off his buckskin shirt. Moments later, he had shed his boots and trousers as well. Natalie sat up to peel

127

his underwear over his hips and drop it around his ankles. Fargo kicked it aside and rested his hands on Natalie's shoulders as she leaned forward to kiss the tip of his erection. She nuzzled the crown of his shaft with her soft, warm lips, then opened them to take the thick pole of male flesh into her mouth. Fargo reveled in the heated sensations her lips and tongue created in him.

After a few minutes he urged her back on the bed and knelt between her widespread thighs. His fingers massaged her, finding the sensitive muscles and kneading them expertly. He moved his thumbs closer to her core and used them to pull apart the fleshy pink lips of her sex. His head dipped down and his tongue speared into her, causing her to utter a little cry and lift her hips from the bed.

"Oh, Skye . . ."

Fargo delved as deep within her as possible with his tongue before replacing it with first one finger and then two. Natalie was drenched with the juices of the passion he aroused in her. Fargo lapped up the dew that beaded on her femininity, running his tongue all along her portal.

He couldn't wait any longer. His shaft was so hard it ached with the need to dip into her. He moved over her, positioning himself, then surged forward with his hips. Natalie moaned as he entered her.

Fargo felt her muscles clasp him in their tight, buttery grip. He stroked in and out of her. Her breasts flattened against his chest as he let some of his powerful weight rest on her. His mouth found hers, and their tongues leaped and thrust against each other in a frenzied duel. Natalie lifted her knees higher and clasped her legs around Fargo's hips, locking her ankles together so that he couldn't have gotten away even if he'd wanted to—a highly unlikely possibility at a moment like this. Fargo kept up the rhythm of his thrusts for long minutes, driving both of them higher and higher on the peak they were scaling. When it was time, he buried himself to the hilt and let his climax wash over him. Natalie spasmed at the same moment, sobbing against Fargo's shoulder at the depth of the pleasure that filled her.

When he had rolled off of her and was sprawled on his back, covered with a fine sheen of sweat, his chest rising and falling as he tried to catch his breath, he said, "When you invited me up here . . . you mentioned something . . . about supper?"

Natalie was snuggled against his side. She laughed. "You men! You never get enough, do you? I give you the best lovemaking you'll ever get, and you want supper!"

"I've got to keep my strength up," Fargo told her. "Unless you want me to go now . . . ?"

Her arms tightened around him. "No," she whispered. "Don't go."

Fargo, Joe Patterson, and Judge Boothe rode along the canyon, followed by two more men from Ophir named Dawson and Rollins, both of them members of the town council. The judge was on horseback this time instead of in his buggy, just in case they needed to move fast. But with five armed men in the group visiting the former Conway claim, Fargo figured Gratton would think twice about starting to throw lead around.

As they came in sight of the claim, Fargo saw that Harry was right: The sluice had been rebuilt. Three men were working at it now. Fargo recognized one of them as Gratton by the hardcase's burly shape.

The three hardmen saw the visitors coming and stepped away from the sluice to pick up rifles. Fargo put his hand on the Henry rifle in its saddle sheath just in case there was going to be trouble. No shots were forthcoming, however. Gratton and his companions just stood there, waiting.

Fargo let Judge Boothe take the lead. On the ride out here, they had discussed the fact that they were going to deal with this situation in a legal manner. Boothe urged his horse forward as the others reined in behind him.

"Gratton, by what right are you here on this land?" the judge demanded immediately.

"The boys and I are claimin' it," Gratton replied.

"Frank Conway already filed on this claim," Boothe said. "He done it legal and proper-like. I seen the papers back in town."

"Conway's dead, and his kids abandoned the claim. We got as much right to it as anybody else." Gratton's attitude was belligerent, but for the moment anyway, he was keeping a tight rein on his temper.

"How do you figure that?"

"There was nobody here when we rode up."

"Conway's markers were still in the ground," Boothe said. Fargo had checked with Dinah and Harry about that this morning. No one had pulled up the claim markers after Conway's death.

Gratton shook his head. "I didn't see any markers." He looked over at the other two hardcases. "Did you, boys?"

"Nope," one of the men said. "Nary a marker in sight." The other man just spat and shook his head.

Gratton had pulled up and disposed of Conway's claim markers, Fargo was certain of that. Anyway, without clear evidence that the claim was being worked, the markers didn't mean all that much. The sluice had been half-destroyed and covered with fallen rock, and only a small part of the cabin that the family had been building still stood.

Gratton gave the visitors an ugly grin. "If you came out here to run us off this claim, you ain't got a leg to stand on. If you was a real judge, you'd know that."

Boothe bristled. "Don't you ever doubt that I'm a real judge! I'll throw your ornery hide behind bars for contempt o' court!"

Gratton looked around and said, "I don't see any court out here. If anybody's in the wrong, it's you fellas for trespassin'."

Fargo spoke up. "You took a shot at Harry Conway yesterday."

Gratton hefted the rifle in his hands. "Just protectin' my property. A man's got a right to do that, don't he, Judge?"

Boothe took off his hat, ran his fingers through his long white hair, and pulled on his beard. He turned and looked at Fargo, and Fargo saw the futility in the old man's eyes. Boothe wanted to take action against Gratton, but his hands were tied by the law.

Fargo walked the Ovaro forward. "Where were you the day Conway was killed, Gratton?"

"Nowhere near here, if that's what you're thinkin'. And I got plenty of witnesses to back up that story."

That came as no surprise to Fargo. Gratton's men would lie for him without hesitation. The only way to definitely link Gratton with the rockslide that had killed Frank Conway was if someone had seen him start it. Lacking such an eyewitness, there was no case against Gratton.

Fargo had known that in his head, but in his heart he had hoped to find something that would break through Gratton's defenses. It was becoming evident that wasn't going to happen, at least not today.

Joe Patterson spoke up. "You'd better watch your step from here on out, Gratton. We'll all be keepin' an eye on you, and if you break one little law, I'll lock you up faster'n you can say Jack Robinson."

Gratton just smirked at him. "I'm a law-abidin' man, Marshal. I been tryin' to tell all of you that ever since the boys and me come to Ophir."

"Let's get out o' here," Judge Boothe said in disgust. "The stink's startin' to get to me."

The party from Ophir turned their horses back down the canyon. As they did so, Fargo and Gratton locked eyes for a second, and that instant was enough for Fargo to see the implacable hatred in the big man's gaze. Gratton was hiding behind the law right now, but he seemed to be saying that the day would come when he and Fargo would finally settle their differences. For his part, Fargo could hardly wait.

When they were out of earshot of the claim, Boothe said, "Well, we didn't accomplish a damned thing by ridin' out here today."

"We put Gratton on notice that we're on to him," Fargo said. "He'll get overconfident and slip up sooner or later. His sort always does."

"Yeah, maybe. How many folks'll get hurt first, though?"

Fargo just shook his head. He couldn't answer that question. All he could do was hope that the day of reckoning would come soon.

When they got back to Ophir the group split up. Fargo went to Omar Sprague's store to talk to Dinah. He waited until she was through helping a customer, then stepped up to her and said, "I wish I had better news."

"You came back safely from confronting Gratton," Dinah said. "That's good news by itself, Skye." She paused, then went on, "He didn't admit anything, did he?"

Fargo shook his head. "He's a cool customer. He had

the audacity to say the law is on his side because the claim was abandoned."

"Well . . . he's right, isn't he?"

Fargo grimaced. "According to Judge Boothe, he is. Joe Patterson put Gratton on notice that he'd better not break any laws, but I don't know what good that will do. For now, everything's going Gratton's way."

Dinah put a hand on his arm. "You'll think of something, Skye. I'm sure of that."

Her confidence was touching but maybe misplaced, Fargo thought. So far Gratton had stymied him.

"Why don't you come to supper tonight?" Dinah went on. "I'm sure Mrs. Lemmon wouldn't mind. She told me last night after you left what a handsome man you are."

Omar Sprague ambled over in time to hear Dinah's last comment. He laughed and said, "Sounds like the Widow Lemmon's set her cap for you, Fargo. Or maybe she's just trying to play matchmaker with you and Dinah here."

Sprague might just be trying to be friendly, but Fargo still didn't like the storekeeper. He ignored Sprague and said to Dinah, "I'd be glad to have supper with you."

Her face lit up with a smile. "Six o'clock sharp. Mrs. Lemmon doesn't like it when people sit down late at her table."

"I'll be there," Fargo promised.

As he left the emporium, he noticed Sprague glaring at him. For a brief moment, Fargo thought he saw the same thing in Sprague's eyes that he had seen earlier in Gratton's—hatred. That didn't make sense, he told himself as he walked up the street. He and Sprague hadn't seen eye to eye on everything since Fargo's arrival in Ophir, but there hadn't been enough friction between them to prompt such feelings on Sprague's part. At least, not in Fargo's judgment. But he had long since learned that it was impossible to crawl into another man's heart and mind and know what he was feeling and thinking. If Sprague wanted to hate him for some unknown reason, then so be it. Fargo wasn't going to lose any sleep over the matter.

That evening, he enjoyed the meal at Mrs. Lemmon's boarding house, and despite his resolve not to lead Dinah on, he found himself sitting in the parlor with her again after supper. It was just a pleasant conversation, though, with no veiled comments about the future or longing looks. Dinah seemed to be coming to the realization that she and Fargo weren't destined to be together. Fargo was relieved about that.

He left the boarding house at a reasonable hour and started toward the livery stable. He had considered and then discarded the idea of stopping at the Top-Notch for a drink. He knew if he did that, he would see Natalie, and then the two of them would no doubt wind up in her bed again, even though they hadn't made any definite plans to be together tonight. It would be better, Fargo decided, to just turn in early for a change.

So naturally, just when he was counting on a quiet, peaceful night, a gun suddenly blasted somewhere nearby.

Fargo stiffened at the sound of the shot. He didn't hear the telltale *whip-crack* of a bullet passing through the air near him, so the shot probably hadn't been aimed at him. Still, his hand went to the butt of his Colt as he readied himself for trouble.

He thought the shot had come from one of the alleys up ahead. As Fargo's keen eyes searched the shadows, he saw a figure come lurching out of an alley mouth into the street. Fargo palmed out the Colt and called, "Hold it!" The man ignored him, staggered a few more steps, and then pitched forward on his face.

Fargo broke into a run, sure that the man had been wounded by the shot he'd heard. Reaching the man's side, Fargo dropped to one knee. He pointed the Colt at the mouth of the alley, ready to return fire if there were any more shots. The alley was dark and silent, however. If the gunman was still there, he was holding his fire and waiting to see what was going to happen next.

Fargo heard the harsh, strained breathing of the wounded man beside him. At least the man was still alive. Fargo grasped the man's shoulder with his free hand and rolled him onto his back. There wasn't much light in the street, but Fargo could see well enough to recognize the pain-twisted face that looked up at him without seeing him.

Harry Conway.

Fargo felt cold fear and hot anger go through him—fear for Harry's life, anger at whoever had done this. Fargo had no choice but to holster his gun and use both hands to try to help Harry. He pulled the young man's coat aside and saw the large dark stain on Harry's shirt, just above his waist on the left side. There was a chance the wound might not be fatal, but Harry needed medical attention as soon as possible.

The pounding of running footsteps made Fargo glance up. He saw a tall, lean figure hurrying toward him, carrying a rifle, and recognized Joe Patterson. "Joe!" Fargo called. "Over here! It's Fargo!" He identified himself so the marshal wouldn't get trigger-happy.

"Fargo!" Patterson exclaimed as he came up. "What's happened here? Who's that?"

"Harry Conway," Fargo said. "He's been shot." Fargo got one arm around Harry's shoulder and the other behind his knees, then straightened from his crouch, lifting the young man with a grunt of effort. "I've got to get him over to Doc Parkhurst."

"I'll go with you," Patterson said, "in case there's any more trouble."

As they hurried along the street toward the doctor's office, Patterson went on, "Did you see who shot him?"

"I didn't see any of it," Fargo answered. "I heard the shot, then saw Harry come stumbling out of an alley. Whoever gunned him down must have taken off, because nothing else happened."

But who would have had a reason to shoot Harry? Fargo asked himself. And what had Harry been doing in that stygian alley in the first place?

Harry was still working for Walt Drummond, Fargo recalled. At the boarding house tonight, Dinah had mentioned something about Harry having some errands to run for Drummond. That was why he hadn't been at supper.

When he got Harry safely in the hands of Doc Parkhurst, he was going to have a talk with Drummond, Fargo decided. And if Drummond didn't like the questions he asked, that would be too damned bad.

Fargo was relieved to see that a light was burning in Parkhurst's office. If the doctor had been out on a call somewhere, Fargo would have taken Harry into the office anyway and done his best to patch up the youngster's wound. Experience had taught Fargo quite a bit about dealing with bullet holes. But it would be better to have Parkhurst tend to the injury. A real doctor had skills and knowledge that Fargo lacked.

Patterson hurried ahead to open the door. As Fargo carried Harry into the building, he saw Parkhurst getting up from behind the desk, a startled and worried expression on his face.

"Fargo!" Parkhurst said. "My God! I heard a shot a few minutes ago, but I didn't think—Is that Harry Conway?"

"It is, Doc," Fargo said. "Where should I put him?"

Parkhurst bustled over to an open door. "Bring him in here and put him down on the examining table. What happened?"

"Gunshot wound, low on the left side."

"It missed the heart and lungs, then," Parkhurst muttered as if thinking to himself. "There'll be some danger of stomach injury, and internal bleeding, of course . . ."

As gently and carefully as possible, Fargo lowered Harry onto the table in Parkhurst's examining room. Parkhurst lit a lamp and turned the flame up as high as it would go, so that its glow filled the entire room. He leaned forward over the table and began using a small pair of scissors to cut away Harry's blood-soaked shirt around the wound.

When Parkhurst had the wound exposed, Fargo saw that it was much as he had hoped: The bullet had passed through Harry's left side leaving a wound that was more than a simple bullet crease, but one that didn't appear to be too deep. Parkhurst said, "Give me a hand here," and he and Fargo rolled Harry onto his right side. Parkhurst cut away more of the coat and shirt. Fargo frowned as he looked at the two bullet holes. The one in the front was larger than the one in Harry's back, meaning that it was the exit wound and the bullet had hit him from behind.

Patterson saw the same thing. "Backshooter," the marshal said.

Fargo nodded. It was possible Harry hadn't had any warning that he was in danger until the gun roared and the bullet struck him from behind. One thing was almost certain, given the circumstances and the darkness of the alley—Harry wouldn't have gotten a look at whoever shot him.

"Hmm, doesn't look too bad," Parkhurst said. "I think I can deal with this if you men want to go look for whoever is responsible."

"That's a good idea," Patterson said. "You comin', Fargo?"

"Damn right." If there were any clues to the backshooter's identity in that alley Fargo wanted to see them for himself.

"Better send word to the boy's sister," Parkhurst called after them as they left the office. "Let her know he's down here."

"Right, Doc," Patterson said.

The shot had drawn the attention of several townspeople, and as Fargo and Patterson went outside, Patterson told one of the bystanders to run down to Mrs. Lemmon's boarding house and let Dinah Conway know her brother had been hurt. The man hurried off. Fargo and Patterson went to the alley where Harry had been shot. Fargo struck a match as he and Patterson stood at the mouth of the alley. Both of them looked at the ground in front of them.

"Lots of tracks," Patterson commented. "Folks use this alley as a shortcut, so I ain't surprised there are plenty of footprints."

Fargo swept his eyes from side to side, studying every inch of the alley. He didn't see anything unusual. When the lucifer burned down, he struck another and hunkered on his heels to take a closer look at the array of footprints. Nothing stood out about them. He saw tracks from hobnailed boots such as most miners wore, along with the marks of shoes and the sort of boots preferred by men who spent a lot of time on horseback, such as himself.

"Anything?" Patterson asked.

Fargo shook his head. "It could have been anybody in town that shot Harry." He straightened from his crouch. "I want to talk to Drummond and see if he knows what Harry was doing skulking around this alley."

Two stores, both of them closed for the night, flanked the narrow lane. Almost directly across the street was the front of the Top-Notch, Fargo noted with a frown. No one in the saloon seemed to have paid any attention to the shot. Raucous piano music came from the place, which might explain the lack of interest. When things were at their rip-roaring best inside the Top-Notch, a gunshot outside might not even be heard.

Fargo stalked toward the Gold Bar. Even though Patterson was taller, with longer legs, he had to hurry to keep up with the Trailsman's pace. As Fargo approached Drummond's saloon, he heard music and laughter coming from inside it as well. Ophir seemed to be in a good mood tonight.

Pushing the batwings aside, Fargo stepped into the Gold Bar. No one paid any attention. The music continued, men kept drinking at the bar, and the poker games going on at the tables never faltered. The shrill laughter of the soiled doves who worked in the place filled the air as the customers fondled them and made lewd comments. Fargo looked around for Walt Drummond and spotted the big, bald saloonkeeper at his customary table in the rear corner.

Drummond had a bottle of whiskey and a glass in front of him. He looked up as Fargo strode toward him, Patterson following behind. The owlish expression on Drummond's face told Fargo that the man was a little drunk. That wasn't going to stop Fargo from finding out what he waned to know.

"Drummond," Fargo asked, "where's Harry Conway?"

"How should I know?" Drummond replied in surly tones.

"He works for you, doesn't he?"

"Yeah, but I don't keep up with the kid every waking minute." Drummond gazed around the room with his bleary eyes. "I don't see him. Why don't you check with that pretty sister of his?"

"I know where he is," Fargo said.

Drummond blinked. "Then why the hell are you asking me?"

"I wanted to know if you sent him to that alley across the street from the Top-Notch."

Drummond didn't say anything in response to that, but Fargo saw something flicker in his eyes. More surprise, maybe.

"What if I did?" Drummond finally said.

"That's where he was shot a little while ago."

Drummond was reaching for the bottle. His hand jerked at Fargo's words, and he nearly upset the whiskey. "Shot!"

Drummond lurched up and out of his chair. He tried to shake off the effects of the whiskey he'd poured down his gullet this evening. "What happened? Is the kid okay?"

"There's a chance he will be," Fargo said. "He's in Doc Parkhurst's office now, having his wound tended to."

"Son of a bitch!" Drummond's voice rumbled like thunder, and at last the people in the saloon were beginning to notice that something was wrong. Heads swiveled as people turned to look toward the table in the corner. "It had to be her, or somebody who works for her! That bitch!"

Drummond's words took Fargo a little by surprise. "What are you talking about?" he asked.

"I had the kid watching the Talmadge woman's place. I heard a rumor that since I told Gratton I didn't want anything to do with him, he was throwing in with her to see that my business was ruined."

Fargo frowned. This was the first he'd heard of any connection, rumored or otherwise, between Natalie and Gratton. The whole thing sounded highly unlikely to Fargo. He thought he knew Natalie well enough by now to be sure that she wouldn't have anything to do with a hardcase like Gratton, and besides, Gratton had his hands full these days with the gold claim that had formerly belonged to Frank Conway.

He didn't bother explaining any of that to Drummond. The odds were that Drummond wouldn't have listened anyway. The man was furious. He pointed a finger at Fargo and said, "You go ask that woman what happened to Harry. She probably spotted him watching her place and had one of her flunkies shoot him!"

Fargo didn't believe that for a second. "You're crazy, Drummond," he said. "Natalie wouldn't—"

"You just don't want to believe it because that bitch has had you in her bed!"

Fargo was getting mighty tired of listening to Drummond refer to Natalie as a bitch. He was just as frustrated by Drummond's insistence on blaming Natalie for what had happened to Harry.

Drummond looked from Fargo to Patterson and back again. "Well?" he demanded. "Aren't you going to do anything about it?" When they didn't respond, he shoved the table aside and started toward them, clearly intending to shoulder them aside. "If you won't do anything," he muttered, "I will!"

Fargo grabbed his shoulder. "Wait just a minute, Drummond!"

Drummond didn't wait. Instead, he swung a roundhouse punch that would have taken Fargo's head off if it had connected. Fargo ducked under it and slammed a short but powerful blow into Drummond's midsection. The punch traveled only six inches or so, but Fargo's fist sank almost to the wrist in Drummond's belly.

Drummond paled and staggered back, bending over from the force of Fargo's blow. The Gold Bar had gone quiet at last, as everyone in the place stared at the confrontation between Fargo and Drummond.

The violence didn't have a chance to go any farther, because at that moment, a rider galloped past in the street outside, and a man's voice was lifted in a frantic shout.

"Murder! Somebody help! Ben's dead! Murder!"

10

Patterson swung toward the door of the saloon. Fargo hesitated a moment, not wanting to turn his back on Drummond if the man was about to pull a gun on him. Drummond was still gasping for breath, though, with one hand flat on the table to support him while the other arm was pressed across his middle. Clearly, despite his size and the impression he gave of being a brawler, he had a weak stomach when it came to getting punched there. Judging that Drummond wasn't an immediate threat, Fargo joined Patterson—and quite a few of the Gold Bar's customers—in pouring out of the saloon and into the street.

Someone had caught hold of the rider's reins and pulled his horse to a stop. Patterson came up to the man, whose chest was heaving as he tried to catch his breath after a breakneck ride, and asked, "What the hell's goin' on here? What's all this about murder?"

"My . . . my partner Ben Harper," the man said. "Claim jumpers shot him this evening. He thought he heard somethin' . . . outside the cabin . . . and went out to take a look around. A minute later, I heard a shot. I ran out . . . Ben was on the ground over by our long Tom. There were two men standin' over him. I yelled at 'em, and they started shootin' at me. It was just blind luck I was able to grab a hoss and get out of there 'fore they ventilated me."

"Did you see who the men were?" Patterson asked, his voice and face grim.

The prospector shook his head. He was middle-aged, not very big, with a scruffy gray beard. "Nope, it was too dark. But I reckon we can maybe figure out who one of 'em was."

"How's that?" Patterson asked.

The man patted the flank of the horse he had ridden into

town. "This hoss belongs to one of 'em. I didn't say I grabbed one of the hosses that belongs to Ben and me."

Fargo's pulse picked up a little. The claim-jumper's horse was the first solid lead they had been able to come up with to the men responsible for the violence in the area.

Patterson said, "Lead that animal over here into the light. I've seen most of the horses hereabouts at least once."

The prospector caught up the reins and led the horse into the light that spilled past the batwings of the Gold Bar. It was a good-looking animal, tall and rangy with a chestnut coat. There was nothing special about the battered old saddle or the saddlebags. The pouch, however, yielded a creased and dirty envelope addressed to Saul Pomeroy.

When Patterson read that name aloud, one of the townies said, "I know that name. Pomeroy's one of the men who ride with Gratton."

Fargo patted the chestnut's shoulder. "I recognize this horse, too. Think back to when we were out at the Conway claim this afternoon, Joe. We saw it there."

"We sure did!" Conway agreed. "It belongs to one of those fellas who was workin' the claim with Gratton."

"They didn't waste any time," Fargo said. "They were so convinced Gratton has us buffaloed that they rode over to that other claim tonight to murder the men there and get rid of their bodies. Then in a few days Gratton would say it was abandoned, too, and move in on it just like he did with the Conway claim."

" 'Cept I rattled my hocks fast enough to ruin that plan," the prospector said.

Fargo smiled and clapped the man on the shoulder. "You sure did." He turned to Patterson. "Joe, we'd better roust out Judge Boothe and ride out there to arrest Gratton's men."

"What about Gratton himself?"

"He'll probably deny knowing anything about the killing," Fargo said. "But I'm hoping we can prod him into doing something rash."

"Sounds good to me. I'll go find the judge."

Patterson hurried off while Fargo said to the prospector, "Can you lead us back to your claim?"

"I'll say I can! I'll do anything to see that those murderin' skunks get what's comin' to 'em!"

Within fifteen minutes, a posse was riding out of Ophir, bound for the claim where the killing had taken place. Fargo, Patterson, Judge Boothe, and the prospector who had escaped from Gratton's men rode in the front of the group. The prospector, whose name was Dunlap, had recovered from his frantic ride into town and was anxious now to see his partner's death avenged.

Before leaving town, Fargo had stopped by Doc Parkhurst's office and found Dinah there, worrying over her brother. Parkhurst, though, seemed to think that Harry stood a good chance of making a full recovery.

"The bullet doesn't appear to have damaged any internal organs," Parkhurst had explained. "I've cleaned and bandaged the wound. Now we just have to worry about blood poisoning."

Fargo nodded, patted Dinah on the shoulder to reassure her, and went back to join the others.

The claim that had been worked by Dunlap and Harper was not far, as the crow flies, from the Conway claim. When the posse arrived there, Fargo called the party to a halt and then he and Patterson rode forward cautiously, rifles in hand. The cabin loomed dark and seemingly deserted, but Fargo knew gunmen could be lurking in there.

When they were close, Fargo and Patterson dismounted and took cover behind some trees. "You in the cabin, come on out with your hands up!" Patterson called. "This is the marshal from Ophir!"

No response came from the cabin. Fargo's sharp eyes scanned the scene and spotted the dark shape lying sprawled on the ground next to the sluice Dunlap and Harper had built. That would be Harper, Fargo decided. The killers had left him lying where he fell.

After a few minutes, Patterson said, "What do you think, Fargo? Are they still in there?"

"I doubt it," Fargo replied. "They probably took off when they realized that Dunlap had gotten away and their plan was ruined. I'll check in the cabin to be sure."

Running in a near crouch, Fargo approached the cabin and ducked through the open door, the Henry rifle ready to spew lead and death if need be. No one challenged him, and when he struck a match he saw that the cabin was indeed empty, just as he had thought. He came out and called to Patterson and the others. "They're gone."

Dunlap dismounted and hurried over to his fallen partner. A quick check confirmed that Harper was dead. Dunlap cursed bitterly. "Those skunks. Those murderin' skunks."

Judge Boothe asked Fargo, "Where do you reckon they went?"

"The first place to look is Conway's place," Fargo said. "They probably went running back to Gratton."

"Gratton can't save 'em now. We got Pomeroy's horse as proof they did the killin'."

Fargo nodded and suggested, "Dunlap, why don't you stay here and see to burying your partner? The rest of us will ride over to Conway's."

Dunlap rubbed his scraggly jaw. "I'd like to be in on the finish, but I reckon I owe Ben a decent burial. And we don't need to delay, in case those bastards who shot him try to get out of these parts."

"My thoughts exactly," Fargo said. He swung up onto the Ovaro and led the posse away from the darkened cabin.

They had to circle back to the stream where the Conway claim was located and follow it north for a couple of miles. Fargo knew the country well by now and had no trouble getting where he wanted to be, despite the darkness. The moon rose, sending a silvery glow washing down over the Sierra Nevadas, and that made the ride a little easier still. In less than an hour, the men from Ophir were approaching the Conway claim.

Fargo lifted a hand to signal a halt. In a whisper, he said, "We'd better spread out and go ahead on foot. They may be waiting for us."

Patterson nodded his agreement. He motioned for the group to split up. One man was delegated to remain with the horses while the others worked their way forward.

There weren't many places to hide, Fargo thought as he studied the scene in the moonlight. There was no cabin except for the partial walls, and those wouldn't provide much shelter. The biggest structure on the claim was the long sluice box.

That was where the shots came from as bullets began to

slash through the night. Fargo bellied down on the ground as muzzle flashes split the darkness. Patterson shouted, "Hunt some cover, boys!", as he ducked behind a tree.

Flame geysered from the barrel of a gun behind the sluice. Fargo aimed for the flash, fired the Henry, then rolled to the side in case the killers tried to return the fire. The posse was spread out over a front about fifty yards wide. Most of the men began shooting. Bullets smacked into the beams and planks of the sluice box. Judge Boothe's old hogleg roared. Fargo continued peppering the sluice with the rifle.

He hoped they could take the men alive and that Gratton was with them. Pomeroy and the second killer—if the second man hadn't been Gratton himself—might implicate Gratton in the murder of Ben Harper if they thought it would help save them from a neck-stretching. Fargo was convinced that Gratton had given the orders for Harper's killing, even if he hadn't participated.

Fargo called over to Patterson, "Keep them pinned down, Joe. I'm going to try to get behind them."

"Be careful, Skye," Patterson said, worry in his voice. "Those boys won't hesitate to gun you down."

Fargo wouldn't hesitate to kill, either, if it came to that. But he still hoped it wouldn't.

He crawled behind a nearby log, came up on hands and knees and made his way along its length. When he reached the end of it, he surged up onto his feet and broke into a run, the Henry held slant-wise across his chest. A couple of slugs smacked into the ground around his feet, but then the posse directed a new fusillade toward the men behind the sluice, forcing them to stop shooting and duck for cover.

Fargo came to the stream and splashed across it. When he reached the other side he flattened himself against the rocky bluff that bordered the creek. Its rugged, irregular face had several protrusions that served as shelter from the flying bullets as Fargo worked his way along it. More than once, a shot came close enough to kick dust and rock splinters into Fargo's face, but he pressed on, unwilling to turn back now.

When he reached the last of the cover, about twenty yards from the place where the bluff curved behind the sluice, he dropped to one knee and thrust the barrel of the Henry around the rocky bulge. From here he had a clear shot at the men holed up behind the sluice. A bullet tugged at the brim of Fargo's hat. He ignored it and fired three times, sending all of the bullets thudding into the side of the sluice just above the heads of the defenders. "Throw down your guns!" he shouted. "Or the next ones will be aimed at you!"

The men were trapped. They couldn't make a break for it, because the rest of the posse was waiting to cut them down if they emerged into the open. But if they stayed where they were, the expert aim of the Trailsman would blow them into rags. Facing the inevitable, one of the men yelled, "Hold your fire!"

Fargo heard the other man curse his companion, and then that second man burst out from behind the sluice, triggering his pistol in the direction of the hidden posse members as fast as he could cock and fire. Fargo led him just right with the Henry and sent a bullet spearing through his thigh. The impact of the slug spun the man off his feet and sent his gun flying through the air.

The first man had his hands up, showing empty in the moonlight. Fargo came out from behind the rock and trotted toward him, covering him all the way with the rifle. Patterson and some of the other posse members converged on the wounded man. Patterson scooped up the revolver the man had dropped.

"Are there just two of 'em?" Patterson called to Fargo.

Fargo used the barrel of the rifle to motion his captive away from the sluice. "Just two," Fargo said. "I got a good look at them. Nobody else was hiding back there."

"And neither one of 'em are Gratton," Patterson said with disgust in his voice.

The wounded man was unconscious. Judge Boothe ripped strips off the man's shirt and used them to bind up the bullet hole in his leg. As Boothe straightened from that task with a grunt, he said, "That oughta hold him until we can get him back to the doc. He'll live to hang, that's for sure."

"Hang!" the first man yelped. "We didn't do anything to deserve hangin'! All we did was shoot at some strangers sneakin' up on our claim in the dark."

Boothe faced him. "Would you be the one called Pomeroy?"

"N-no. That's Saul over yonder, the one who was shot."

"You been with him all evenin'?"

"Sure, right here on the claim."

"That won't work," Boothe said with a shake of his head. "You see, we got Pomeroy's horse to prove he was at the claim of a couple of gents named Dunlap and Harper earlier tonight. Harper was shot and killed, and Dunlap got away by the skin of his teeth. I'm chargin' you boys with the murder of Harper."

"Damn it, I didn't kill nobody!" Like a weasel, the captive was quick to turn on his wounded comrade. "That was Saul's doin', every bit of it!"

"And who ordered the two of you to kill Harper and Dunlap?" Fargo asked.

The prisoner gave him a frightened look and said, "I don't know what you're talkin' about, mister."

Fargo wasn't surprised to find that the gunman was more afraid of Gratton than he was of the law. "Where's Gratton?"

"Haven't seen him since this afternoon."

"He didn't light out when you two jaspers showed up and told him Dunlap had got away?" Boothe asked.

"I don't know what you're talkin' about," the prisoner said again.

Boothe spat on the ground in disgust. "We ain't gonna get anything outta this no-account polecat, not yet, anyway. Maybe his tongue'll get a mite looser when he's facin' the gallows."

Patterson ordered, "Let's get 'em on some horses and head back to town."

A few minutes later, the group was on its way. The wounded prisoner, Saul Pomeroy, was only half-conscious, but he was tied into the saddle so that he couldn't fall off the horse. Posse members surrounded Pomeroy and the other hardcase as they rode, so there was no chance of them making a getaway.

At the front of the party, Judge Boothe said to Fargo, "What do you reckon Gratton will do when he hears we got these two locked up?"

"I don't know," Fargo replied. "He may think he can

count on them keeping quiet and not implicating him in Harper's death, but that would be a mighty big chance for him to take. I think it's more likely he'll ride into town with the rest of his men and try to free them."

"And when he does, we'll be waitin' for them," Patterson put in.

"That's right," Fargo said with a nod. "If Gratton comes calling, we'll be waiting."

The arrest of the two men caused a sensation in Ophir. The next day, to make sure that everything was done legally, Judge Boothe empanelled a grand jury that heard the testimony of Pete Dunlap and examined the evidence in the form of the horse and the letter that belonged to Saul Pomeroy. It didn't take long for the grand jury to indict Pomeroy and his companion, Art Brindle, for the murder of Ben Harper.

Judge Boothe banged his gavel on the table in the outdoor courtroom and said, "Trial is set for tomorrow mornin' at nine o'clock. Marshal, take the prisoners away."

At least two men would be standing guard around the clock outside Joe Patterson's tack room where Pomeroy and Brindle were locked up. Patterson wouldn't be putting these prisoners to work in the stable. He didn't want to take any chances on them escaping.

Fargo was an interested observer to these goings-on, and when they were over, he headed to Doc Parkhurst's office. Harry Conway had been moved into Parkhurst's bedroom to recuperate from his wounds. He was pale and weak looking when Fargo came into the room and found Dinah sitting on the edge of the bed beside her brother, but at least Harry was conscious.

"Doc says you're going to pull through," Fargo greeted the young man. "That's good news. Do you have any more for us?"

Harry shook his head. "I don't know what you mean, Mr. Fargo."

"I'm hoping you can tell us you saw who shot you last night."

"I'm sorry," Harry said with a sigh. "I sure didn't. I didn't know anybody else was around until I heard the gun and felt the bullet."

Fargo turned a chair around and straddled it, tossing his hat on the foot of the bed as he did so. "That's what I was afraid of. So you don't have any idea who did it?"

Harry shook his head again.

"Skye, I'm not sure that Harry is up to a lot of questions—" Dinah began.

"No, that's all right," Harry said. "I'm feeling a mite peaked, but not too bad. I just don't think I can help you find who did this, Mr. Fargo."

"Drummond told me he had you watching the Top-Notch for any sign of Gratton," Fargo said.

"That's right. Somebody told him Gratton was working with Mrs. Talmadge now."

"Did he say who told him that?"

"Nope."

"And you didn't see Gratton anywhere around the Top-Notch?"

"No, sir, not at all. I didn't really believe that Mrs. Talmadge would have anything to do with somebody like Gratton. She seems like a pretty nice woman—for somebody who owns a saloon."

Fargo agreed with that sentiment, but he didn't say so in front of Dinah. Instead, he asked, "Have you come across anything to link Drummond to your father's murder?"

Harry frowned. "No, I haven't, and that sort of bothers me. I was so convinced he had something to do with it, but the other day he told me he was sorry about what happened to Pa. He sounded like he meant it, too. Mr. Drummond blusters a lot, but after being around him for a while, if I didn't know better I'd almost say he's really not a bad sort."

Fargo ran a thumbnail along his bearded jawline and tugged on his right earlobe as he thought about what Harry had just said. If Harry had misjudged Walt Drummond, maybe Fargo had, too. Maybe the friction and rivalry between Drummond and Natalie Talmadge had colored his thinking, Fargo mused. Was it possible that Drummond hadn't had anything to do with the fire at the Top-Notch or Frank Conway's murder?

Fargo could accept the latter possibility more easily than he could the former. Gratton could have been acting alone in Conway's death, but who else in Ophir had a reason to burn down the Top-Notch? No one that Fargo could think of—except Walt Drummond.

Harry sighed. "I guess I won't be doin' any more investigatin'."

Fargo smiled and said, "Not for a while. All your time's going to be spent recovering from gunshot wounds." He got to his feet and picked up his hat. "But don't worry, you two. I'm still going to get to the bottom of your father's death and everything else that's been going on around here."

"I know you will, Skye," Dinah said. She took his hand and pressed it for a second.

As he stepped out of the room, Fargo hoped that she wasn't misplacing the confidence she had in him.

Stopping in the doctor's front office, he said to Parkhurst in a quiet voice, "If somebody wanted Harry Conway dead enough to shoot him, they could try to finish off the job."

Parkhurst nodded. "I know. I've already spoken to Marshal Patterson about having a man keep an eye on the place. And there's a pistol in my desk drawer, too."

"You know how to use it?"

"I don't like to," Parkhurst said, his voice grim, "but I know how, you can count on that."

"Good," Fargo said with a nod. "Because I'm counting on you to keep that boy safe, Doc."

He started out of the office, but Parkhurst stopped him by asking, "What's going to happen with those two men you captured last night?"

"They go to trial first thing in the morning. It shouldn't take very long."

"And then?"

"Hear that hammering? Joe and some of the other men are already building the gallows."

That evening, Fargo was having dinner with Natalie Talmadge in her room on the second floor of the Top-Notch. Natalie looked as beautiful as always, but a hint of worry lurked in her eyes.

"What do you think is going to happen, Skye?" she asked as she looked at Fargo over a glass of champagne. "Gratton won't just let his men be tried and hanged, will he?"

"I wouldn't think so," Fargo replied. "He's got to be worried that if they go to trial, they'll testify he ordered them to kill Harper and Dunlap and steal their claim."

"Will he try to break them out of Joe Patterson's livery stable?"

"It's a possibility." Fargo didn't really want to talk about Gratton and all the trouble around Ophir. He hadn't gotten to spend much time with Natalie in the past few days, and there was no way of knowing how much time they would have together in the future. When they were finished eating, he suggested they take their champagne and move to the love seat in the corner.

Natalie agreed. She settled herself close beside Fargo and rested her right hand on his muscular left thigh. With a sigh she laid her head on his shoulder. "I wish we could stay like this forever," she said in a quiet voice.

"Sometimes I do, too."

Natalie laughed, but the sound had a faint quality of regret. "But you're the Trailsman," she said. "You have to ride on and see what's on the other side of the hill, or the mountain, or the river."

"Something like that," Fargo agreed.

"You're enough to drive a woman to distraction, Skye Fargo. Even a woman like me, who's never had any real . . . domestic leanings, I suppose you could say. All a woman has to do is look at you, and she starts thinking about a home, and a family . . ." Natalie tossed back the rest of her champagne. "Oh, hell, what's the use?" She moved her hand to his groin and began massaging the length of male flesh that stiffened and grew there. "I'm going to take what I can get of you, as many times as I can get it."

That sounded good to Fargo, too. He set his champagne aside and turned to take her into his arms.

That was when gunshots and galloping hoofbeats sounded in the street outside.

Fargo's instincts took over. He sprang to his feet, and his hand went to the butt of his gun. He hurried to the window and looked out in time to see a man on horseback disappearing at the far end of the street. The rider had a pistol in his hand and was still whooping and triggering gunshots as he went out of sight.

"What in the world?" Natalie asked.

"Looked like somebody letting off steam," Fargo said. "I've got a hunch it was more than that, though."

"So now you have to go see what it was," she said with a sigh.

Fargo gave her a quick grin as he picked up his hat and headed for the door. "I'm afraid so."

Something made him duck through the opening quickly and swing the door shut behind him. No sooner had he done that than he heard a champagne glass shatter on the other side of the panel. With a rueful shake of his head, Fargo headed for the stairs.

When he reached the street he saw a crowd in front of Sprague's Emporium. Hurrying down there, he heard Sprague talking in a loud, angry voice. "Right through the window!" Sprague was saying. "Busted it all to hell with that rock!"

Fargo shouldered his way through the crowd and reached Sprague just as Joe Patterson and Judge Boothe came up from different directions. "What's going on here?" Patterson asked.

"That lunatic who raced down the street shooting off his gun threw a rock through my front window!" Sprague said. "And it had a note tied onto it. Look!"

Sprague thrust out a piece of paper. Judge Boothe took it and squinted at it in the poor light. "I ain't got my readin' spectacles," he said. "Can't quite make it out." He passed the note on to Fargo.

"It's from Gratton," Fargo said as he scanned the crudely printed words. "He's giving us until tomorrow morning at sunrise to turn his men loose. If we don't . . ." Fargo looked up at the others. "He says he'll burn the town down around our ears."

A frightened muttering went through the crowd. "He'll do it, too," Sprague said. "Ever since he's been around here, he can't stand being crossed."

Patterson asked, "Are you sayin' we should let them two go, Mr. Sprague?"

The storekeeper shook his head. "Hell, no. Gratton's run roughshod over all of us for too long. It's time somebody stood up to him."

"The smart thing might be to get the prisoners out of here," Fargo suggested. "We could take them to Sacramento and hold them for trial there. I'll take them there myself if that's what everyone wants."

"It wouldn't do any good," Sprague said. "Gratton would still attack the town because we had the gall to arrest a couple of his men in the first place." Sprague looked around at the gathering of townspeople. "I say we go ahead and hang 'em tonight, so they'll be waiting on the gallows for Gratton in the morning!"

Fargo stared at the storekeeper. "A minute ago you sounded like you thought we should let them go to try to save the town."

"What kind of town will we have here if Gratton can get away with whatever he wants?" Sprague's voice rose. "The only language his kind understands is violence! We have to fight back, and we can get in the first blow by hanging those men!"

"Hold on, hold on," Judge Boothe said. "Trial's already set for nine o'clock tomorrow mornin'."

"Gratton will have the town in flames before then."

As much as Fargo hated to agree with Sprague, he had a feeling the storekeeper was right. And getting the prisoners out of town probably wouldn't help, either. Gratton would still take his bloody vengeance on Ophir.

"Forget about hanging anybody," Fargo said, his voice quiet but powerful and commanding attention. "We have to get ready for Gratton."

"What do you mean?" Patterson asked.

"I don't know how big Gratton's gang is, but there are fewer of them than there are people in town. We can defend ourselves against him."

"But Gratton and his men are outlaws," Sprague protested. "Most of us are just normal people. We're not fighters."

Fargo looked squarely at him. "If you want to hang on to your town, you'll have to fight."

From the edge of the crowd, a voice Fargo recognized as Walt Drummond's spoke up. "Fargo's right," Drummond said, surprising him a little. "Let's get some barricades up and arm everybody we can find. We'll give Gratton a warm welcome!"

Fargo looked over at Drummond, and the big saloonkeeper grinned at him. Fargo couldn't help but return the grin. It looked like Drummond had forgotten about that punch in the belly.

In times of bad trouble, old grudges had to be put aside. This was one of those times, Fargo realized as Natalie Talmadge came up with a shawl wrapped around her shoulders and said, "Drummond's right. We'll make Gratton wish he'd never come to Ophir!"

A shout of agreement went up from the crowd. Judge Boothe turned to Fargo and said, "You've worked with the Army before. You reckon you can set up the town's defenses by sunrise?"

"We don't have any choice," Fargo said. "We've got to be ready—or tomorrow's the day Ophir dies."

Fargo, Judge Boothe, Joe Patterson, and everyone else in Ophir worked all night, sleeping little if any. By the time the eastern sky was beginning to turn gray with the approach of dawn, a compound of sorts had been constructed in the middle of the broad main street. Furniture had been dragged from the buildings and piled in the street to form breastworks that stretched from one side of the street to the other at both north and south ends. More lumber had been dumped outside the barricades and soaked in coal oil so that it would burn easily when the time came. Riflemen were stationed behind the false fronts of several of the buildings, ready to pick off the outlaws when Gratton's gang came storming into town. The rest of the citizens were behind the barricades, even the wounded Harry Conway, who had been carried from Doc Parkhurst's office and placed on a pallet behind a water trough. Harry gripped a gun in his hand, and Dinah waited with him, a shotgun at her feet. If the battle reached their position deep within the stronghold, it would mean that things had gone very badly for the townspeople, but in that event at least the two of them would be able to put up a fight.

Fargo thought Gratton would come from the north end of town. He was waiting at the barrier there, along with Judge Boothe. Joe Patterson was stationed at the other barricade, commanding the men there just in case Gratton attacked from that direction.

"I reckon I understand now how those ol' boys down in Texas at the Alamo felt," Boothe commented as he checked the loads in his Dragoon Colt.

"Except they were outnumbered by Santa Anna's army," Fargo said, "and there's a lot more of us than there is of Gratton and his men."

"Yeah, but Gratton's bunch is used to fightin' and killin'." Boothe looked around at the townspeople congregated within the barriers. "These folks ain't. I wish we had more guns and ammunition, too. If Gratton gets in here, it'll be a damned bloodbath."

"That's why we have to keep him out."

Boothe glanced up at the sky. "Won't be long now. Sun'll be up in a half hour or so."

Fargo stiffened as the judge's words soaked into his brain. Gratton's note had threatened an attack on the town if the prisoners were not released by sunrise. All they had was Gratton's word for that, however, and Gratton had shown himself to be pretty tricky . . .

"Everybody down!" Fargo called, but the words weren't out of his mouth before guns began to blast. From the corner of his eye, Fargo saw a couple of the townies stagger and fall, blood welling from bullet wounds. Another volley rang out, fired from a long distance but with deadly accuracy. Bullets sang around the heads of the townspeople as they ducked for cover.

Gratton had some of his men up in the hills above the town, firing down into it to provide a distraction and cut down some of the defenders. The next step would be a full-fledged attack. As he crouched behind the barricade and reached for one of the coal oil–soaked torches he had prepared earlier, he heard the drumming of hoofbeats.

Fargo snapped a lucifer into life and lit the torch, then stood up and threw it at the pile of lumber in front of the barrier. A bullet whipped past his head as he did so. The blazing torch hit the lumber, and the wood caught instantly. The pile turned into an inferno, throwing a flickering, hellish light all over this end of town.

At the other end of the compound, Joe Patterson did the same thing, tossing a burning torch onto the makeshift bonfire. Now the defenders had plenty of light to shoot by.

Fargo snatched up his Henry as he saw men on horseback, a dozen or more of them, come boiling out of the predawn gloom. He brought the rifle to his shoulder and began firing as fast as he could work the Henry's lever. Bullets sprayed out from the muzzle of the weapon.

He heard a rattle of gunfire from the south and risked a glance over his shoulder. Patterson and the men posted at that end of the compound were shooting at another group of riders. Gratton's gang was bigger than he had thought, Fargo realized, big enough for the leader of the renegades to split his forces and smash into Ophir from two directions at once.

For better or worse, the fight was on.

11

The group of charging renegades had to split up to go around the bonfire burning in the middle of the street. As they did so, Fargo saw at least two of them go tumbling out of their saddles. But Ophir's defenders were suffering casualties, too. A man who stood behind the barricade a few feet to Fargo's right staggered back and dropped his gun. Blood welled from the hole in the center of his forehead as he collapsed.

Another of Gratton's men fell as the fire from the riflemen stationed behind the false fronts of the buildings began to take its toll. Fargo looked for Gratton himself, but didn't see the burly renegade. The Henry's magazine ran dry. Fargo ducked below the top of the barricade to reload.

As he did so, one of the outlaws drove his horse forward and smashed into the barrier, toppling a couple of the pieces of furniture that had been stacked up to form it. Fargo threw himself out of the way of a falling wardrobe that shattered into kindling as it struck the ground. He rolled over in time to see the hardcase clambering through the gap he had created in the barricade by sacrificing his horse. Lying on his back on the ground, Fargo drew his Colt and fired twice. The slugs ripped upward through the outlaw's body and flung him backward.

Fargo came up on his knees, holstered the revolver, and started thumbing cartridges into the Henry's loading gate. He heard Judge Boothe shout, "Take that, you consarned polecats!" The judge was firing the Dragoon Colt two-handed, fighting the recoil that tried to send the heavy revolver's long barrel upward after every shot.

Fargo flicked a glance toward the other end of town and

saw that Joe Patterson and his men were putting up a good fight. None of Gratton's men had gotten through the barricade at that end of the street. Obviously, Gratton was willing to spend the lives of his men to achieve the ends he wanted, but he didn't have an endless supply of men. Fargo risked a look over the barrier and saw that four of the outlaws were down and the others were pulling back.

He still didn't see Gratton. The renegade leader was hanging back, waiting to see what was going to happen. Fargo wouldn't put it past him to desert his men once he saw that they weren't going to be able to breach Ophir's defenses.

The shooting died away as the outlaws fled. The townspeople began looking around, checking on their dead and wounded, and asking each other if it was over.

Judge Boothe began reloading the Dragoon. He said to Fargo, "Well, they turned tail and ran."

"They'll be back," Fargo said. He wasn't sure how he knew that, but his instincts told him it was so.

Boothe frowned. "There was more of 'em than I thought there'd be, but we hurt 'em bad, Fargo. Must've downed at least half a dozen of 'em. Gratton ain't fool enough to think he can fight a whole town, is he?"

"A man's pride can goad him into doing things that don't make any sense." Fargo shook his head. "I just don't think we've seen the last of Gratton."

That wasn't the prevailing attitude in the rest of the makeshift stronghold, however. As Fargo walked along the street, he heard people congratulating each other on defeating Gratton's gang. A few of the defenders had been killed and a few more wounded, but considering that a pitched battle had just been fought here, the losses had been light.

One of the wounded was Walt Drummond. The saloonkeeper was sitting on the edge of the boardwalk while Natalie Talmadge knelt beside him and tied a bandage around his bloodied upper arm. Fargo stopped for a second in surprise when he saw that, then grinned and shook his head and moved on. Fighting side by side for their lives sometimes did strange things to folks, made them see things about other people, both good and bad, that they might never have seen otherwise. Fargo had just witnessed that for himself, the way the two formerly bitter rivals were now getting along.

He came to the horse trough where Dinah and Harry Conway were waiting. Both of them were all right, Fargo saw with relief.

"A few bullets came close," Dinah said in answer to his question of how the battle had gone here, "but not too close."

Harry was propped up with his back against the thick trough. He lifted the gun in his hand and said, "I wish I could've got a shot at them. To pay them back for what they did to Pa."

Dinah put a hand on his shoulder. "You just rest, Harry. You shouldn't even be out here."

"You wouldn't have wanted to be trapped in Doc's house if Gratton had managed to set the town on fire," Fargo pointed out. "At least out in the open you've got a chance."

"Gratton's gone now, isn't he?" Dinah asked. "That's what everyone is saying, that he gave up the fight and took off."

"I don't know," Fargo said. "I'm not convinced he doesn't have something else up his sleeve."

Reassured that Dinah and Harry were all right, at least for the moment, he moved on, heading for the barricade at the south end of town. When he got there, he found Doc Parkhurst slapping a bandage on a bullet crease on Joe Patterson's leg while Patterson sat on the ground.

"It's nothing to worry about," Parkhurst assured the marshal. "When this is over, though, you may have to stay off that leg for a day or two while it heals up."

"It's over now, ain't it?" Patterson looked up at Fargo. "Gratton's bunch took off for the tall and uncut."

"It looks that way," Fargo admitted. Several minutes had passed with no further sign of the renegades. Maybe everyone was right to be optimistic . . .

"Here they come again!" someone shouted from the north end of town.

Biting back a curse, Fargo turned and raced for the northern barricade. Men were scrambling into position to repel an attack, but a wicked volley of gunfire drove them.

As Fargo came up to the barrier, he saw Judge Boothe stumble and go down.

In an instant, Fargo was at Boothe's side. The judge waved him away, saying, "I'm all right, dagnab it! They just nicked me!"

Fargo saw blood on the white shirt under the judge's dusty black suit, and he was afraid the wound wasn't just a nick. There was no time to make sure, though, because a glance past the barricade told Fargo that Gratton had concentrated his forces and was throwing all of his remaining men into this attack. At least two dozen outlaws were charging the barrier on horseback, blazing away with rifles and pistols as they came.

Fargo fired through a niche in the barricade and saw one of the renegades drop. Suddenly, the group of riders split apart. The outlaws peeled away to the sides, and Fargo saw that one man had been riding right behind the phalanx. That man threw something toward the barricade with all his strength. That was his last act on Earth, because in the next instant a slug from Fargo's Henry punched through his body and toppled him from his horse.

Widening in horror, Fargo's eyes followed the thing the man had thrown through the air. It was a small keg with something trailing from it that sparked in the dawn shadows. Fargo knew the keg had to be full of blasting powder, and the sparks came from a fuse.

The bonfire had died down. The keg was going to clear it and land either on the barricade or just inside it. Fargo knew he had only split seconds to act. "Back!" he bellowed as the Henry sprang to his shoulder and he lifted the barrel. "Everybody get back!"

He fired, missed, levered the repeater, fired again. The keg blew apart with a blinding, ear-splitting blast as Fargo's bullet sizzled into it.

The explosion was close enough to pick Fargo up like a giant hand and toss him backward. It blew down part of the barricade, too. Fargo rolled over a couple of times before he came to a stop lying facedown in the street. He had lost the Henry. As he lifted his head and blinked eyes that stung from the smoke of the blast, he saw riders pouring through the gap in the barrier. His hand went to his hip and found the Colt still in its holster. Palming out the evolver, he fired twice and was rewarded by the sight of one of the renegades tumbling from his saddle.

"Get 'em!" Judge Boothe shouted. The fighting jurist was on his feet again despite his wound, pouring lead into the attackers from the old Dragoon Colt. A few yards away, Walt Drummond and Natalie Talmadge stood together on the boardwalk, Drummond firing a handgun while Natalie took aim with a rifle. In the middle of the street, Joe Patterson limped forward, the gun in his hand blazing. Beside him came Doc Parkhurst, his accurate shots proving that he had told the truth when he assured Fargo he knew how to use a gun. Harry Conway was firing over the top of the water trough. Dinah knelt beside him, tracking one of the outlaws with the shotgun in her hands before she let go with both barrels. From a window on the second floor of the Drake Hotel, the clerk fired a pistol down into the melee, and beside him was a lean, bushy-haired man, the Russian cook, also using a pistol. All up and down the street, the people of Ophir fought a desperate, last-ditch battle for their town.

And Fargo was in the middle of it, surging to his feet, snapping off a shot, twisting, firing again. He spotted Gratton, one of the last men through the blown-apart barricade. As Fargo lined the Colt on him and pulled the trigger, the hammer fell on an empty chamber. With a grimace, Fargo jammed the revolver back in its holster and stooped to slip the Arkansas toothpick from the hidden sheath in his boot. He lunged toward Gratton.

Gratton saw Fargo coming and threw a shot at him. The bullet whined past Fargo's ear. Fargo leaped, slamming into horse and rider and toppling both. Gratton kicked free of the stirrups and rolled away. The collision had knocked the gun out of his hand, Fargo saw. But Gratton had a knife, too, and he came up swinging it.

Fargo parried the swiping blade. Steel rang together and sparked. Gratton tried to kick Fargo in the groin. The Trailsman twisted and took the blow on his thigh, slashing at Gratton at the same instant. Gratton jerked back, but not before the tip of Fargo's blade raked down his left arm and trailed a bloody gash behind it. Gratton roared in pain and furry and came at Fargo again, slashing madly with the knife.

Fargo gave ground, drawing Gratton on at the same time.

Gratton lunged and lost his balance. Fargo kicked one of his ankles out from under him, driving Gratton to the ground. Fargo landed on top of him, thrusting the Arkansas toothpick toward Gratton's chest. At the last instant, Gratton grabbed Fargo's wrist and stopped the knife's deadly plunge.

At the same time, Fargo grasped the wrist of Gratton's knife hand. They were locked together like that with Fargo on top for a second or two, then Gratton put all his strength into a heaving roll that sent Fargo over and brought the renegade atop the Trailsman. Gratton was heavier, and he put his weight behind his efforts to bring his knife down into Fargo's chest.

The muscles of Fargo's arms and shoulders bunched and corded as he held off Gratton's assault. It was a stalemate, as neither man was strong enough to overpower the other. The tip of Gratton's blade danced only inches in front of Fargo's eyes. The red glare of flames reflected off the cold steel.

"Now . . . I'm gonna . . . kill you . . . Fargo!" Gratton gasped.

After everything that had happened to Skye Fargo in an eventful life, he was damned if he was going to let a bastard like Gratton end it. Calling on reserves of strength from deep inside him, Fargo arched his back and bucked up with his arms and legs, and Gratton's weight was suddenly gone, flung off to the side. Fargo rolled and came up on his knees at the same time as Gratton, but his thrust was a split-second faster. The long, heavy blade of the Arkansas toothpick buried itself in Gratton's chest. Gratton made one last try for Fargo with his fading strength, but Fargo knocked the knife aside. Gratton rocked back, his knees bent double underneath him, then sprawled on his side with the handle of Fargo's knife still protruding from his chest.

Fargo swayed a little, his chest heaving from the desperate fight he had just won. He became aware that the gunshots had stopped, and when he looked around he saw a scene of carnage. The bloody bodies of the renegades were spilled everywhere, littering the street. The people of Ophir began to gather around. Quite a few of them were bloody, too, but they were still on their feet. They had won. Gratton's gang was wiped out.

"Skye!" With that worried cry, Dinah Conway came running to him. Fargo stood and caught her in his arms, hugging her and assuring her that he was all right.

"Now it's over," he murmured. "Gratton's paid for what he did to your father."

To his shock, he heard a rasping, blood-choked laugh. Looking down, he saw that Gratton wasn't dead. Life was fading fast in the big man's eyes, but he was still alive, and he was laughing at them.

Fargo let go of Dinah, went to a knee, and rolled Gratton onto his back. With a hideous grin, Gratton said, "You . . . still think . . . I killed the gal's pa."

"If you didn't do it yourself, you ordered it done," Fargo said, his voice cold.

Gratton shook his head. "No . . . you're wrong . . . Fargo. I took over . . . the claim . . . but I didn't have nothin' to do with . . . killin' Conway . . ."

His dying breath went out of him with a grotesque rattle, and he sagged lifelessly on the ground.

For a long moment Fargo stared down at Gratton, then with a sigh he got to his feet. From beside him, Dinah said, "Skye . . . what he said . . . that couldn't possibly be true, could it? I . . . I thought Gratton was the one who killed Pa."

"So did I," Fargo said.

But now he wasn't so sure.

Ophir made a remarkable recovery from the battle that had almost ended its existence. In less than a week's time, the dead had been buried, the damage had been repaired, and the wounded were recuperating under the diligent care of Doctor Parkhurst, who had sustained a wound of his own, a bullet through the left forearm that had missed the bone. He made his rounds wearing a black silk sling to support that arm. Joe Patterson assured him that it made him look dashing.

The two prisoners, Saul Pomeroy, and Art Brindle, were tried and found guilty of Ben Harper's murder, even though they testified that they were just following Gratton's orders. In accordance with the laws of the State of California, both of them were hanged by the neck until dead. That should have been the end of it.

There was nothing to hold Fargo here. Nothing except the nagging thought that he hadn't gotten to the bottom of everything, as he had promised to do.

Taking the word of a dying man was a tricky thing to do. Fargo talked it over with Judge Boothe, who told him that a dying declaration was considered proof in a court of law. On the other hand, had Gratton been so twisted and evil that he had lied right up until the end? Maybe insisting that he hadn't had anything to do with the avalanche that killed Frank Conway had been Gratton's way of playing one last trick.

Fargo didn't know, and that uncertainty kept him from riding on.

It wasn't Natalie Talmadge keeping him in Ophir, that was for sure. The temporary alliance between Natalie and Walt Drummond showed signs of becoming a permanent one. They seemed to have put their hard feelings behind them, and Drummond had been to the Top-Notch for supper a couple of times in the past week. Fargo watched the budding romance with a bemused attitude. He was fond of Natalie and wanted only the best for her. Drummond really wasn't such a bad sort, and if he made Natalie happy, that was all right with Fargo.

But there was still the question of the fire that had come close to destroying Natalie's saloon. That was another nagging, unanswered question in the back of Fargo's mind.

The election for mayor had been postponed due to the battle with Gratton's men. Finally, Election Day dawned clear and beautiful in the Sierra Nevadas. Since Omar Sprague and Doc Parkhurst were both running, it was decided to hold the election in the Drake Hotel, as it was neutral ground. Fargo figured he didn't have a vote, since he wasn't a permanent resident of the town, but he was on hand to watch the proceedings, as were Judge Boothe and Joe Patterson. No matter what the outcome, no one was going to be able to say that it hadn't been a proper, legal election.

It didn't take long for Fargo to discover that watching an election was one of the most boring things on earth. When Dinah showed up with box lunches for the election watchers, he decided to walk with her back to Sprague's Emporium.

"The store's closed today because of the election," she explained as she and Fargo strolled down the boardwalk, "but Mr. Sprague asked me to go through some of his accounts and see if I can straighten out his bookkeeping. I used to do that for my father back in Illinois."

"Sprague's lucky to have you working for him," Fargo commented.

"Yes, well . . ." Dinah looked down at the boardwalk. "Sometimes I think he's a little too happy to have me at the emporium."

Fargo stopped and frowned. "What do you mean?"

Dinah seemed uncomfortable as she explained, "I think he'd like to court me."

"What? But he's old enough to be your—"

"My father, yes, I know. But it's not unusual for an older man to take a young woman as his wife."

Fargo had to admit that such things weren't unusual at all, especially on the frontier where there was always a shortage of women. An older, more successful man was often able to claim a considerably younger woman as his bride. But not Dinah, Fargo thought. She wouldn't ever marry a pompous, arrogant windbag like Omar Sprague.

Fargo couldn't say that, however, not without interfering in Dinah's life, and he had no right to do that. No matter what he thought of Sprague, if she decided that she wanted to be with him . . .

"Of course, I'd never do that," Dinah went on, confirming Fargo's hunch. "Not with Mr. Sprague, anyway. I don't even like him."

Fargo was glad to hear that. He linked his arm with Dinah's and walked on down the street with her.

She used a key from the pocket of her dress to unlock the door of the emporium. "Why don't you come in and keep me company while I work on the books?" she suggested.

That didn't sound much more exciting than watching the election, Fargo thought, but he smiled and said, "Sure." At least here he would have the pleasure of Dinah's company.

He sat on the counter at the rear of the store while she worked at a desk behind it, spreading ledgers open in front of her. As her pen scratched on the pages, she talked about how much better Harry was doing. "We're thinking about giving the claim a try again, now that Gratton's gone," she said. "It'll be a lot of work, but we feel like we owe it to Pa."

"If you're going to do that, be sure it's because that's what you want," Fargo advised, "not because you feel like you owe it to anybody."

"You're right, of course. But we do want it." She looked up at Fargo and grinned. "After all, we came to California to get rich."

Fargo chuckled. The lure of gold was always there for most people, put away sometimes but never totally forgotten.

"Now, that's odd . . ." Dinah said a moment later. She frowned down at the ledger in front of her.

"What's odd?" Fargo asked.

Dinah set the pen aside and turned the book so that Fargo could see it. "As far as I can make out, Mr. Sprague owns a considerable amount of property here in Ophir besides the store. I thought this was his only business."

Fargo leaned forward to peer at the ledger. He frowned as he saw the property boundaries that were listed and tried to figure out exactly where they were located along the main street. After a moment, he said in surprise, "Those are saloons. Damned if it doesn't look like Sprague owns nearly all the saloons in town except the Top-Notch and the Gold Bar."

And just like that, he had the answer to one of the questions that had been bothering him, the question of who would stand to gain besides Walt Drummond if fire destroyed the Top-Notch.

It was as if floodgates had opened in Fargo's brain. All along, Natalie and Drummond had insisted that they were innocent, that the other one was to blame for all the trouble between them. Now Fargo saw that it could have just as easily been a third party stirring the pot, someone who could come out ahead by keeping Natalie and Drummond at each other's throat until they destroyed each other.

Someone like Omar Sprague.

"Son of a bitch," Fargo breathed. At least that part of the puzzle made sense now. "It was him all along. It was Sprague . . ."

Dinah looked past him, her eyes widening, and she said, "Skye."

165

He heard the metallic sound of a pistol's hammer being drawn back, and an icy voice said, "Don't move, Fargo."

Fargo stiffened. Sprague had the knack of moving quietly, so quietly that even the keen ears of the Trailsman hadn't noted his arrival in the store. He wasn't alone, either, because a second later an anxious voice asked, "What are you going to do, Omar? He's figured it out."

"Shut up, Tom," Sprague said. "Let me think." He added, "You be still, Dinah. I don't want to shoot you. That's the last thing I want."

"We have to kill them," Tom Harlin urged. "Fargo knows what we've been doing."

Despite the tension gripping him, Fargo summoned up a chuckle. "That's right, Harlin. I know you and Sprague have been working together to cause trouble for Drummond and Natalie Talmadge. What did Sprague promise you for helping him? The Gold Bar? Don't you know better than that, Harlin? He'll just double-cross you."

"Shut up!" Sprague snapped.

Fargo's thoughts were whirling as more and more of the pieces fit together. "It was Dinah, wasn't it?" he said. "You weren't content with trying to lock up all the saloon business in Ophir. You wanted her, too, but you decided that to get her you had to cut her off from her father and brother. So you killed Frank Conway, and then you either shot Harry or had Harlin do it. Harlin had a grudge against him to start with."

Harlin's voice had an angry hiss to it as he said, "Damn it, Omar, you told me no one would ever know what I did! If you hadn't lost your head over that girl—"

"Shut up!" Sprague said for the third time. An edge of hysteria crept into his tone. "All of you just shut up!" After a moment he regained some control and went on, "Don't worry about Fargo, Tom. He's just guessing."

Dinah said, "But he's right, isn't he? You did it, Mr. Sprague. You killed my father, and you had Harry shot." She stood up, the ledger still in her hand. "I hate you!"

"No, Dinah, don't say that," Sprague pleaded. "I'm going to be a rich man. I . . . I can make you happy, the happiest woman in California. I just had to make you turn to me, so that I could . . . could help you . . ."

"You bastard!" Dinah screamed.

166

And with that, she threw the ledger at him.

Fargo dived off the counter, twisting in midair and shoving Dinah to the floor as he reached for the Colt with his other hand. A gun blasted somewhere close behind him, but the bullet smacked harmlessly into the store's rear wall. Sprague's aim had been thrown off as he instinctively ducked the ledger. Now Fargo was crouching behind the counter, the walnut grips of the Colt smooth against his palm as the barrel of the gun came up. Another slug hit the counter, chewing splinters from it. Fargo fired. The bullet drove into Omar Sprague's midsection, doubling him over. The gun in Sprague's hand blasted once more, but this time the shot went into the floor at his feet as he collapsed.

That left Tom Harlin to deal with. The little pocket pistol he'd yanked from under his coat gave a spiteful crack. Fargo heard the whine of the bullet close beside his ear. He triggered a second shot, but Harlin was moving, throwing himself behind some shelves full of merchandise. Fargo's bullet missed.

Fargo ducked lower behind the counter as Harlin fired again. Dinah said, "Skye—!" Fargo motioned for her to stay down. He began edging toward the end of the counter. He knew the shooting would draw plenty of attention, and a crowd would be arriving soon. Harlin's only chance was to kill Fargo and Dinah, then slip out of the emporium through the back and join the curious townspeople who would be showing up at any minute. That way the deaths of Fargo, Dinah, and Sprague would remain an unsolved mystery. It was either that, or run for his life. So the gambler didn't have much time. He would have to play his cards now or fold his hand . . .

Fargo heard a rush of footsteps as he reached the end of the counter. He threw himself forward, landing on his belly in the open as Harlin made a rush at the other end of the counter. Harlin tried to stop when he saw Fargo. He jerked the gun toward the Trailsman.

The Colt bucked in Fargo's hand as he fired twice, bracketing the single shot that Harlin got off. The gambler's slug smacked into the floor to Fargo's left. Both of Fargo's bullets bored into Harlin's chest, driving him backward. He crashed into a wall where shovels, hoes, axes, and other tools were hung on pegs. As he collapsed, several of the tools fell down around and on top of him. He didn't move again.

Fargo got to his feet and started forward, intending to check on Sprague and Harlin and make sure both men were dead. He had taken only a step when Sprague rolled over, his face contorted in pain and insane rage. He lifted the pistol in his hand.

A shotgun roared from behind the counter, and at that range, the double charge of buckshot blew Sprague's head apart. Dinah lowered the smoking muzzles of the weapon and said, "That was for Harry and my father . . . and for me."

She placed the empty shotgun carefully on the counter, then her eyes rolled up in her head and she fainted dead away.

The doors of the emporium slammed open, and several men poured into the store, led by Judge Booth, Joe Patterson, and Doctor Parkhurst. They stopped and stared at the carnage, and Fargo said, "No matter how the votes turn out, Doc, it looks like you just won the election."

Fargo sat on the Ovaro and looked at the newly built log cabin. It was sturdy, and a tendril of smoke came from the stone chimney. Over by the sluice box, Harry Conway was explaining how it operated to Igor Malakoff, who had decided to give up cooking and become a gold miner. Dinah sat in the buggy next to Fargo's horse, and Judge Boothe was with her.

"I got the papers drawn up," Boothe said. "Ol' Igor was happy to come in for a third share. I'll sure miss the sort o' grub he could whip up, though."

"Harry can't work the claim by himself," Fargo said, "and Dinah's going to be busy in town running the emporium."

"I still don't feel completely right about taking it over," Dinah said.

Boothe snorted. "Shoot, ain't nobody deserves it more'n you, Miss Dinah. And since Sprague didn't have no relatives to claim it, the court—meanin' me—had to decide how to dispose of his estate. I know you was raised in a general store back in Illinois, so if anybody can make a go of it, it's you."

Dinah looked at Fargo. "I could use some help running it, you know."

Fargo grinned and said, "Can you imagine me in an apron?"

"Well . . . no, I honestly can't." She sighed. "So this is goodbye, isn't it, Skye?"

"Call it so long," Fargo told her. "I might be riding back this way someday, you never can tell. I'd sort of like to see how Ophir turns out now that it's got a judge and a marshal and a mayor, not to mention an honest storekeeper."

"It'll be growin' by leaps and bounds," Boothe said. "Thanks to you, Fargo."

"I may have lent a hand," Fargo said, thinking of the way the townspeople had fought for their community, "but that's all. Ophir belongs to the people who live there."

"Where do you belong, Skye Fargo?" Dinah asked softly.

Fargo gazed around at the mountains, the majestic pines reaching for the heavens, the clear, fast-flowing waters of the streams, the eagles free-wheeling through the deep-blue sky, and said, "Out here somewhere, over the next horizon."

With a wave of his hat over his head, he heeled the Ovaro into a fast trot and went to look for it.

LOOKING FORWARD!

**The following is the opening
section from the next novel in the exciting
Trailsman series from Signet:**

**THE TRAILSMAN #249
Silver City Slayer**

*Virginia City, 1859—Where the Good Book clears
the path to salvation, and the Book of Fargo
provides the means for survival.*

Skye Fargo turned his lake-blue eyes toward Davidson
Mountain, where the mining town of Virginia City was
stuck precariously to the rocky side. The town wasn't much
to look at, considering that it was one of the richest in
the territory.

The preacher was standing beside Fargo. His name was
Alfred Nelson, and he was a short, compact man who had
worn nothing but black suits during their entire trek from
Missouri. The suits hadn't traveled well, and the one he
was wearing now was so thickly coated with alkali dust that
it looked almost gray instead of black.

Nelson was a funny kind of a preacher, Fargo thought,
because under the suit coat he wore a pistol that he knew
how to use. He hadn't turned a hair on the trip out from

Missouri when they'd passed the bones of animals, and sometimes of people, who'd come before him and died on the way. He'd just spouted off some scripture about Ezekiel in the valley of dry bones and wheels within wheels high up in the air. It didn't make a lot of sense to Fargo, but it seemed to mean something to the preacher. Now he was quoting scripture again.

" 'A city that is set on a hill cannot be hid,' " Nelson said. " 'Neither do men light a candle and put it under a bushel, but on a candlestick; and it gives light unto all that are in the house. Let your light so shine before men, that they may see your good works, and glorify your Father who is in heaven.' Book of Matthew, chapter five, verses fourteen through sixteen."

Fargo thought about Virginia City with all its whorehouses, opium dens, gambling halls, saloons, and billiard halls. He thought about the thieves, robbers, whores, gamblers, brawlers, and killers who were among the boomtown's inhabitants. And he thought about the abandoned mine shafts with dead men lying at the bottom. Some of the men had fallen in when they were drunk or when the shafts had been covered with snow. A lot of the men hadn't fallen in by accident, however. Not unless they'd tied their hands and feet together first.

Fargo looked down at the little preacher and said, "The men up on that hill wouldn't know good works from Adam's off ox. Book of Fargo, chapter one."

The preacher kicked at the dirt, sending up a puff of dust.

"I don't believe I'm familiar with that book," he said.

"Wouldn't expect you to be," Fargo told him. "But it's the truth anyhow."

"Don't matter a bit to me whether it's the truth or not," Leo Harp said. "That's the place we've been looking for, so let's get ourselves on up there while it's still daylight."

The other men standing around them all muttered their agreement. They weren't a bad bunch, Fargo thought. They just didn't know what they were getting into.

Take Harp, for instance. He was a tall, wiry man who'd been a school teacher back in Missouri, or so he said, but he'd given up that profession to look for silver on a Godforsaken mountain in the middle of nowhere. What kind of a chance did he have? Not much of one, in Fargo's estimation.

Nelson was different. The preacher wasn't planning to strike it rich or even work in the mines. His idea was to bring the word of the Lord to as rough a crew of men as there was anywhere in the West. He thought all he had to do was find a corner to stand on, bring out his Bible, and start in on the preaching. If he did that, he was convinced that people would flock around him.

"They'll be hungry for the message of the Good Book," Nelson told Fargo early in their journey. "I'll have a crowd of a hundred before I say ten words."

Fargo thought he'd be lucky to have a crowd of ten by the time he'd said a million words. Virginia City wasn't known for the spirituality of its citizens. They were too busy grubbing silver out of the guts of the mountain to do much praying. And if they weren't working, they were spending their money on things that were far from the works of God.

What Nelson believed or did wasn't any of Fargo's business, however; no more than it was his business what happened to any of them. There was Cal Edwards, a big bear of a man, who'd given up barbering for the lure of silver; Lane Utley, a tightly-knit man burned brown from the sun, who'd been a farmer and decided he was tired of following a mule and a plow; Waymon Carter, who'd never worked a day in his life from what Fargo gathered although he claimed to have been a justice of the peace; Jim Taylor, a shopkeeper, who'd been perhaps a bit more honest than the others and told Fargo that he was headed west to avoid the war that was sure to come.

"It'll tear Missouri apart," he said, "and I don't want to be there to see it. I'd just as soon go out West and get rich digging up the ground. The war will never get to Nevada territory."

He was probably right about that, Fargo thought, but living in Virginia City was about as dangerous as being in a war. You were just as likely to get killed as if you were on the field of battle, except you'd never see your enemy, who'd back-shoot you or wait in an alley some dark night and knife you before you even knew he was there.

Fargo didn't think Taylor was afraid of danger, though. It was what would happen to his friends and neighbors that bothered him, and if he couldn't do anything about it, at least he didn't have to be a part of it.

"Well?" Harp said. "We've come all this way. What are we waiting for?"

Fargo was a trailsman, and he'd been hired on to guide the men back in St. Jo. He'd gotten them to Nevada safely, across the plains and the great desert, and he'd done a good job of it. Hadn't lost a one of them. Now they were in the Carson Valley and they could see their goal, clinging to the mountain high up in the distance.

Fargo didn't blame them for being eager to get there, though he thought they'd all be better off if they gave up on any idea of striking it rich and just hired out to work in the mines. There was always a job there for a man with a strong back and a willingness to work down under the earth in the damp darkness of treacherous tunnels.

For his part, Fargo would be glad to call an end to the journey. He'd taken half of his fee in advance, but the rest of it was due on their arrival in Virginia City. He planned to keep it in his pocket and get out of town as soon as he could. There were more ways to lose your money in a town like that, and more people who'd like to take it than Fargo could count.

"All right," he said, "let's get moving. We'll want to take it easy, though. By the time we pass through Gold Hill and get up to Virginia City, we'll be so high that we'll have to watch out for birds flying by our heads. Some people don't find it easy to breathe up there."

"We'll be fine," Harp said. "Come on."

He had always been the most impatient of the men, the first one to awaken in the mornings, urging everyone to get up and get started. Fargo had never minded. The quicker they got where they were going, the quicker he'd be paid.

He took the lead, and the men followed him, heading for their vision of El Dorado.

It was late afternoon when they reached the town, but they could hear the stamp mills pounding and the steam engines whistling. The noise never stopped in Virginia City. There were times during the day and even the night when the earth shook and the buildings shivered from underground explosions, but only newcomers were bothered. Everyone else had gotten used to it.

The town staggered up the mountain. Buildings that faced the street were propped up in back with high foundations or sometimes just stilts so flimsy that it seemed the blasting underneath would send them sliding down the mountainside. There were still some people living in tents, though no one lived in caves or dugouts or coyote dens as some had in the earliest days of the town's great growth spurt.

Goats, the town's source of milk, roamed the streets along with stray dogs, miners, cardsharps, rounders of all kinds, and maybe even an honest citizen or two. There were wagons everywhere: wagons loaded with supplies going to the mines, wagons full of ore, wagons coming up from California with hard goods and food, including canned oysters and sardines. Nothing was too good for the rich citizens of Virginia City.

They threaded their way through the crowded streets. No one paid them any mind. Everyone in Virginia City was used to strangers, and a few more didn't matter much one way or the other. Besides, in a boomtown, or any other town in the West for that matter, it was better not to pay much attention to strangers. Curiosity was likely to get you killed.

Fargo called them to a halt in front of the Iron Dog Saloon.

"All right," he said. "This is as far as I go. We'll all go inside and conduct our business, and after that you're on your own."

The preacher looked at the batwing doors. There was laughter coming from inside the saloon, and music, too. It wasn't church music, that was for sure.

"I don't think I much want to do business in a place like that," he said. "It looks like a den of thieves to me."

"No more than any other place in this town," Fargo said.

"He's right," Harp said.

It seemed he was always the one who spoke up first, Fargo thought. Maybe it had something to do with being a teacher. No one seemed inclined to carry on the conversation, not even Nelson, so Fargo dismounted and looped the reins around the hitching post.

Fargo stepped up on the boardwalk and approached the batwings when he saw that there was a large iron dog sitting beside them. It was painted black, but there were rust spots showing through the paint here and there.

"Good-looking dog," Cal Edwards said, reaching over to pat it on the head. His huge hand covered the top of the head easily.

All the others, except Fargo and Nelson, patted the dog when Edwards was finished.

"Go ahead," Carter said to encourage them. "Might bring you good luck."

"I don't believe in luck," Nelson told him. "I believe in the Good Book."

"Not to mention that hogleg you have strapped on you," Taylor said.

"Never mind about that," Nelson said. "There's no conflict there. The Lord helps those who help themselves."

"What book of the Bible is that from?" Fargo asked.

"It's from a different book. One by a man named Poor Richard."

"You mean Benjamin Franklin?" Harp asked.

"One and the same. He had some wise things to say, even if he wasn't as good a Presbyterian as he should have been."

Lane Utley turned and spit tobacco into the street. He wiped his mouth on his sleeve and said, "Are we gonna stand out here talking until it gets dark, or are we gonna go in there and get our business done?"

"Come on," Nelson said, and pushed through the doors.

They were greeted by the sound of music from a badly out-of-tune piano. The air was thick with the smell of smoke, spilled beer, and cheap whiskey. There was a smoke cloud up around the high ceiling, and there was the muttering talk from men sitting at the tables or standing at the bar. The gamblers didn't even look up when they walked in, and the saloon girls were all occupied by men who were pawing them. Nobody cared that a group of strangers had just walked in.

Nobody, that is, expect a tall woman in a feathery, flouncy dress that was tight at the waist and low at the top. She had red hair piled up on her head, and her high, full breasts pushed out over her neckline. She had a wide, generous mouth and clear green eyes. She was quite pretty, and Fargo wondered if she was new at her work. There was none of the hardness he would have expected to see in the face of a woman who'd worked in a saloon for more than a few months.

"Welcome, boys," she said. "I don't believe I've seen you in the Iron Dog before."

Nelson's face was as red as a hot brick. He opened his mouth to speak, but no words came out. Fargo wondered if he'd ever met a real sinner before.

"Our first time," Fargo said. "Looks like a mighty nice place."

He was just being polite, because the Iron Dog wasn't nice at all. It was hastily thrown together from whatever materials were available. The floor was rough, and the long mirror in back of the bar was cracked in two places. The piano music was about as bad as any Fargo had ever heard.

"Nothing but the best," the woman said. "My name's Marian."

"Fargo," the Trailsman said. "Skye Fargo."

The woman gave Fargo an appreciative look, taking in his tall body from head to boots.

"Any kin to the Wells-Fargoes?" she asked.

"Not as far as I know," Fargo said.

"Doesn't matter. Everybody's welcome in the Iron Dog. If you're here for the mining, I hope you all strike it rich. If you're not, well, enjoy your visit to the Iron Dog before you move along."

Marian turned and went to stand by the piano player, a little man dressed like the preacher. The piano itself was pockmarked with holes, and Fargo wondered what had caused them. He also wondered if Marian was going to sing, but she didn't seem inclined to. She was just positioning herself so that she could keep an eye on the room. Besides, thought Fargo, no one could sing in tune with that awful piano.

Fargo looked around the smokey room and saw a table in the back, near a wall. It looked like a good place for a private talk, and he started toward it, motioning for the others to follow him.

He sat down, and the other men pulled up chairs. Utley, Carter, Taylor, and Harp were all holding mugs of beer, having taken advantage of Marian's greeting to go to the bar for a drink. Harp had an extra mug for Fargo, and he handed it across the table.

Fargo took a swallow. It wasn't as bad as he'd expected, so he took another. Nelson watched them drink without any show of disapproval, but he clearly wished they'd get their business done so he could leave.

Fargo set his mug on the table and said, "Time to settle up. You all know what we agreed on."

"We do," Nelson said. "I've been holding the money."

He reached inside his suit coat and pulled out a leather pouch, shielding his movement from the rest of the room. He set the pouch on the table softly so that it wouldn't clink and advertise its contents. Then he pushed it across to Fargo, who stuck it in his shirt just as surreptitiously as Nelson had removed it from its original hiding spot. It was all done so smoothly that no one in the room noticed what had happened, and that was the way Fargo wanted it.

"I'll buy you fellas a round," Fargo said. "And then it's time for you to do whatever it is you came here for."

"I appreciate the thought," Nelson said, "but I'll just go on my way now. I don't hold with drinking."

He stood up and reached across the table to shake Fargo's hand. He had a strong hand and a firm grip.

"May the good Lord be with you, Fargo," he said. "And all the rest of you."

"The Lord helps those that help themselves," Fargo said. "Book of Fargo."

Nelson grinned. "I see you've added a new verse. Or maybe I should say that you've stolen one."

"If you're going to steal, steal from the best," Fargo said. "And I reckon Ben Franklin was one of the best. Good luck to you, preacher."

"Luck doesn't have a thing to do with it," Nelson said. "The Good Book does. Remember?"

"I remember," Fargo said, and Nelson left them with a wave and a smile.

"As for me," Utley said, "I'll take all the luck I can get. And I'll take that beer, too."

Everyone else had a beer, and when they were finished, the men began drifting away one by one. Utley left first, then Harp, then Edwards. Carter and Taylor stayed for another round, then shook hands with Fargo and went out the batwing doors. Fargo thought he might as well be leaving, too. He'd have to find somewhere to spend the night, and the next morning he'd be on his way back down the mountain.

He was halfway to the doors when three men came through. They were big, bigger than Fargo, and two of them were swinging wooden clubs. The other one had a shotgun. They didn't look like men who'd come to have a peaceful drink, and Fargo suddenly wished he'd left a little earlier.

It might be turning into a long night.